HOT WATERS

By

Erica Lyon

Erica Lyon

FOGGY WINDOWS BOOKS

FW

Overdrive

Scarborough, Maine

HOT WATERS

This is a work of fiction. All the characters and events portrayed in this book are fictional, and any resemblance to real people or incidents is purely coincidental.

A Foggy Windows Books Original

Foggy Windows Books
P.O. Box 2358
Scarborough, ME 04070-2358
www.foggywindowsbooks.com

ISBN: 1-930947-03-8

Cover Design by: Lightbourne
Cover Illustration by: Bob Swingle at Lightbourne
Book Design and Typesetting by: Desert Isle Design, LLC

First Printing February 2001

Printed in the United States of America

Dedication:

To my husband, Steve, for his love and understanding;

To my mentors, Kris and Dean, for their support and friendship;

To all three for believing in me, even when I didn't believe in myself;

Thanks.

Prologue

Aleksandr Rezhnenko stood on the deck of the trawler, his hands clasped behind his back. The butt of his pistol rested in the vee formed by his arms, and his feet rode the rolling deck with ease. He could smell the rank odor of the open holds. They had thrown over the spoiled fish, watching as the great white devoured the stinking mass, and the holds still stood open. They would have to close them soon, against the coming storm.

Martin Green clung to the rail, a few feet in front of Rezhnenko, sweat running down his face. Green's fishing boat was tied up alongside the trawler. His first mate waited at the rail of his ship, straining to hear the exchange. Rezhnenko stared from one to the other, weighing his options. He knew the Americans had tried to cheat him. It was only a question of who would take the blame.

"It was a mistake, Captain. I apologize. We were in a hurry; afraid we would miss our meeting. The rest of the merchandise was just misplaced."

Rezhnenko stared at him until Green dropped his eyes to the briefcase at his feet. Krushkin and the Petrov brothers, the trawler crew, had retreated to the wheelhouse where they were carefully avoiding any contact with either man. This was none of their affair, and they clearly had no desire to get between their captain and the Americans.

The bay was quiet, and the rain forest of the Olympic Peninsula was an impenetrable blackness that surrounded them.

Rezhnenko continued staring, watching Green sweat. He felt the power he held over the man, and the anxious eyes of Green's first mate following his every move.

"And if I had taken your word, and not checked it? What then?"

Green glanced up, his expression a mixture of hope and dread. "You would get your merchandise. I swear it."

"How?" The single harsh syllable made Green jump as though he had been lashed, knocking the briefcase off the deck, onto the boat below. The deck rolled as a swell moved across the bay, and he clutched at the rail.

Rezhnenko didn't move.

"I would do whatever was necessary." Green shrugged elaborately, but the gesture did not disguise the fear-sweat that coursed off his body.

"I wonder if you would." Rezhnenko's voice carried a note of curiosity. But he didn't have the time to indulge it.

He stepped toward Green and clapped a meaty hand on his shoulder. "We have done much business together over the years, you and I. We have made a lot of money."

Green's eyes lit with relief at the trace of affection in Rezhnenko's voice.

With one swift, sure motion, Rezhnenko brought the gun from behind his back and fired a single shot into the American's temple. Green didn't even have time to register surprise before the life left his eyes.

Chapter 1

Matthew Carpenter stepped through the bedroom door of his apartment, and into chaos. Drawers open, clothes strewn around the room, suitcases pulled off the top shelf of the closet.

"My God, Sara. What happened?"

His wife stood at the foot of the bed. Her dark eyes glared at him, and she planted her fists on her slender hips. "I'm packing. What does it look like? We have to leave in the morning."

She slipped past him, her hip banging against his, and grabbed an armload of shirts from the open drawer of the cheap upright dresser. "There's frozen lasagna in the oven. It'll take about an hour." She stuffed the shirts in an open duffel bag. "By that time I should be packed."

She made two more trips to the closet and the dresser, brushing past Matt, elbowing him out of her way. With the drawers standing open, there was barely room for her to pass him in the narrow room. The bedroom window was open, the blinds angled to allow the summer evening breeze to cool the stuffy room. Matt could hear the muffled roar of traffic on Highway 101, a block to the west.

She started past him again. He reached out and grabbed her arm, stopping her. He put his other hand under her chin, forcing her face up, until their eyes met.

"You mean to say that all this is because you're packing?" He glanced around the room. It looked vaguely dirty in the twilight filtered through the cheap plastic blinds, in desperate need of the coat of paint he kept promising. He dismissed the thought and turned back to Sara. "Do you have any idea what you're doing?"

Anger and resentment flashed between them. They had been together long enough to know each other's weak spots. Both of them stubborn and proud, they stared at each other, mouths hard, eyes grim. Neither wanted to back down.

Sara wrenched her arm from his grasp. "I've packed your clothes often enough. Just let me get this done," she snapped.

Matt still held her chin, unable to look away. Her dark curls tumbled around her shoulders, released from the tidy ponytail. Her cheeks were flushed, and her skin held a faint sheen of perspiration. A muscle twitched at the corner of her jaw causing a faint tremor against the palm of his hand.

What was it, he wondered, about his wife's temper that was such a turn on? Why did her flashing eyes and grim mouth make him want her so badly, he ached? He gave up trying to decide if it was the fire of her emotion, or the challenge of getting past the wall of anger.

Slowly, daring her to resist, to pull away, he lowered his mouth to hers.

The world moved in slow motion as he pressed his lips to hers. Her mouth was hard, unyielding, but he persisted. He planted tiny, gentle kisses around the tight corners of her mouth, and brushed his lips against the harsh line of hers.

He was rewarded, as he knew he would be, by a softening of her mouth, a rush of warmth, and the feel of her full lips against his. Her mouth opened slightly, allowing his tongue to play over the softness of her lips, the sharp edges of her teeth, the rough surface of her tongue.

Matt loosened his grip on Sara's chin. He trailed his fingers along her jaw line, and caressed her earlobe. He could feel her pulse behind her ear. Already her heart was hammering, responding as his mouth held hers.

He threaded his fingers in her hair, pulling her head back and looking into her eyes. They no longer flashed, but instead smoldered with the stirring of her desire. The sight of her, knowing she wanted him, sent his own arousal even higher. He could feel an erection straining at the buttons of his tight jeans.

His free hand began to roam her body, sliding over the firm planes of her back, dropping down to cup her bottom. He loved the feel of her, the way her cute little butt fit in his hand, the way her body pressed along him. He squeezed, and felt her arch, pushing her crotch against his. Only a few inches shorter than Matt, she had long legs, and they fit together perfectly.

The heat of anger that had been between them shifted, and the heat of passion replaced it. Their bodies, accustomed to each other, knew the places to touch and be touched. Sara's arms wrapped around Matt's neck, and she nipped at his bottom lip, her sharp teeth holding and pulling, but not biting. It sent a wave of pure pleasure through Matt to stab at the straining buttons of his jeans.

She slid one hand up to play with the hair at Matt's collar. She moved the other hand to the front of his shirt, barely brushing against the outline of his nipple.

At the touch, Matt groaned. He buried his face in Sara's neck, alternately nipping and licking. He could taste the salt of sweat and sea spray on her skin, the residue of their day's work aboard *Excelsior*. Her hair smelled of diesel fuel, and ocean and shampoo. It was a heady mixture — the faint memory of Sara's fragrance after her morning shower, mixed with the smells of the boat — and it drove him wild.

Matt slid his hand from Sara's hair and wrapped his arm around her, pulling her even closer, molding her slim body to his. Her breasts were crushed against his chest, her crotch pressed to the bulge in his jeans. Electricity flowed between their bodies, a never-ending current that ran through his veins and ignited a fire deep inside him.

Matt pulled back from Sara's neck and once again found her mouth. Her lips were soft, swollen in imitation of her other, still hidden lips.

"God, you smell good." It was true. Matt had never thought of diesel fumes as sexy, but right now, mixed with sweat and sea spray, it was the most erotic scent he had ever known.

Sara laughed. "You must be crazy, Matthew Carpenter! I'm sweaty and stinky, and I reek of diesel, and probably dead fish, too." She sighed as he caressed her back, then slid his hand around to cup her breast. "But if this is what happens, maybe I'll just put high-test in my perfume bottles from now on."

Her back arched, and she pressed her breast into his open palm. He closed his fingers around the soft flesh, squeezing and stroking. With an impatient tug, he pulled her T-shirt loose from the waist of her jeans, and snaked his hand underneath to tease her rigid nipples. Somehow, she had already shed the constricting sports bra she had worn to work.

Sara's hands were all over him now. She ran her fingernails down his back and yanked at the tail of his shirt. Matt twisted, loosening the shirt where she pulled, and she quickly dragged it over his head. She flattened her hands against his back, her nails digging into his shoulders.

Once free of the shirt, Matt returned his attention to Sara. Her shirt was bunched at her neck, exposing her naked breasts. He loved to look at them, to watch the tips darken and harden when he touched them. Even more, he loved the feel of them in his mouth, the way they leaped and responded to the touch of his lips and tongue. He teased himself with the thought for a moment, then put thought into action.

Her nipple seemed to press into his mouth, as though begging for his attention. He rolled his tongue around the edges, then flicked it across the top, savoring the tremor he felt pass through Sara. Carefully, he took the taut flesh in his teeth, tugged gently, and began to suck.

Sara bucked and moaned, and Matt could feel the heat rising from her skin. She rubbed her mound against Matt's bulging jeans. With trembling fingers, she reached for his waist.

The feel of her hands against the skin under the waist of Matt's jeans was torture, pure and simple. She was driving him mad, and he was loving every minute of it. She skimmed a finger beneath the top button, tickling and teasing his navel. She tugged at his jeans, and they settled a little lower on his hips.

She fumbled with the button, as Matt's lips and tongue and hands continued to tease her nipples. She managed to open one button, then two and three, and then she had him in her hand, her fingers wrapped tightly around his throbbing shaft.

Matt's knees buckled at her touch, and he grabbed her to keep from falling. Definitely time, his desire-fogged brain said, to find a flat surface, any flat surface, before they both fell over.

Dragging Sara with him, Matt staggered to the edge of the bed. Sweeping aside the duffel, the piles of clothes, and God-knew-what-else, Matt cleared the bed, and pushed Sara down. He pulled her shirt over her head, and grasped the waist of her jeans.

In one quick motion, Matt unzipped her jeans and skinned them down her long legs. She was naked now, except for a wisp of delicate nylon panties, a sexy delight hidden beneath the sturdy denim of her jeans. Her skin was flushed with desire, and he could clearly see the swollen lips he had imagined earlier.

He lowered himself next to her, reaching to slide his hand across the slippery nylon. Sara moaned, and pressed herself against his palm. Her breathing was ragged, and he could see the trip-hammer rhythm of her pulse in the veins of her neck.

Sara reached for him, her fingers closing around him once more, and Matt had to grit his teeth to keep from exploding then and there. *Wait,* he told himself. *Be patient.* This was for both of them, and Sara needed time.

Matt forced himself to slow down, to think of anything but what Sara was doing with her busy hands. He concentrated on Sara, carefully removing her panties, stroking her long, limber legs. Brushing the trembling patch between them, he ran his hand up one thigh and down the other.

But Sara wouldn't let him slow down. Busy hands tugged at his briefs, stripping them from him, then tickled and teased, rubbed and stroked and squeezed, until Matt's breath came in great shuddering gasps, and he couldn't hold back any longer.

He raised himself over her, holding himself suspended for a moment longer. Her eyes begged for him, and her hands pulled at him, guiding him toward her.

Then he was inside her, hard flesh against soft, fire meeting fire, until it threatened to consume them both. He lay still for a moment, feeling her body tense around him, squeezing him, urging him on. And he responded, moving slowly at first, then faster.

She matched him, stroke for stroke, thrust for thrust, her body straining against his. Her back arched, pulling him deep inside, straining to hold him even tighter.

It was a force of nature, powerful, wild and unstoppable, like a wave, building far out to sea, and rolling inexorably toward the shore. Sara rode the crest, her body bucking and arching, and she pulled Matt with her. Together, they tumbled over the top, felt the wave break and foam and run up the shore, its power ebbing as it gathered itself to retreat and form again, somewhere far out to sea.

Matt rolled aside, taking his weight off Sara. His skin was slick with sweat, and his heart raced. It had been like this, wild and overpowering, since the very first time. It still astounded him, and scared him a little.

Chapter 2

Cradling Sara in his arms, Matt pulled her head against his chest.

Outside, the traffic had slowed as twilight deepened to evening. The breeze that ruffled the blinds now held a chill. Sara's breath was soft and warm on his cooling skin, her body smooth and sleek. He slid his hands along her back and sides.

It was, he realized with a start, what he did every trip. Each time, before he left, he made love to Sara and held her close. He stored memories — sights, sounds, smells — to keep him company in his narrow bunk aboard *Excelsior*. He saved little pieces of Sara to keep away the loneliness of the vast Pacific until he could come home to her.

But this time would be different. Instead of memories, he would be sailing with the real Sara tomorrow. He didn't know whether to be excited or terrified of the prospect. He knew he loved Sara more than anything in his life, but having an inexperienced hand aboard could be a disaster.

"Mmmmm," Sara snuggled closer, her lips peppering his chest with tiny kisses. "You smell good, too." She drew a deep, contented breath, releasing it slowly across his chest.

"You always smell good to me," she continued, drawing little circles around his navel with her fingernail. It tickled, though Matt was too relaxed to really care. "You smell like you. Nobody else smells that way. It's a mixture of all the things you are — the boat smells and the yard smells when you cut the grass, and the coffee on your breath, and something that I can't even identify, I just know it's you."

She dragged her finger up his stomach, making his muscles twitch in response. "I think I could pick you out of a crowd with my eyes closed. You just smell, I don't know, right somehow. I can't explain, I just know it."

Matt rolled to face her, pulling her close. The two were one, a tangle of arms and legs, intertwined and inseparable. He knew what she meant, he had experienced it, too. But it wasn't any mystery. The only thing he remembered from his required biology class was that smells were nature's way of getting people together. But it was more fun to believe it was something special, just for them.

The buzzing of the oven timer broke the mood and sent Sara scrambling for her T-shirt. Pulling the wrinkled shirt over her head, she trotted into the kitchen and silenced the timer.

Matt sat up slowly, shaking off the stupor that had overtaken him.

Sara was, unfortunately, right about needing to pack. He was ready, of course, but he had stalled her packing, hoping he would find some way that she didn't have to go.

"It needs a few more minutes," Sara called from the kitchen. He heard the oven door slam, and the sound of her bare feet on the worn kitchen linoleum. "I'm just going to take... " Sara's voice paused when Matt dashed past her into the bathroom and turned on the water. " ... a shower!" she yelled, following him into the tiny bathroom.

Matt grinned at her. He was naked, and she wore only the wrinkled "I love Newport" T-shirt and the contented air of a woman recently loved. She peeled the shirt over her head, poked him in the ribs, and squeezed past him while he was distracted.

She beat him into the shower, but that guaranteed nothing. Matt slid the flowered plastic curtain back, and stepped into the tub behind her. She was adjusting the spray, turning the water hotter than he liked, but he wasn't going to give in.

"Hey!" Sara slapped at his hand that reached for the soap. "I got first dibs."

"Ah," Matt snaked his other arm around her and gained possession of the slippery bar. "But I was here first."

"Only a technicality," Sara said, turning to face him. Water streamed through her hair and down over her face and body. She shook her head slightly, sending a spray of water droplets from the ends of her dark hair. "Besides," she continued, "I want to wash my hair first, anyway."

The faint smile that curved her mouth gave the lie to her indifferent tone. It was a game they both knew, one that had endured from the earliest days of their marriage. At first they couldn't stand to be apart for the time it took to shower. Over time it became a loving game they sometimes played after sex.

Knowing the next move, Matt rubbed lather into Sara's bath sponge and began scrubbing her back. The floral scent of her shampoo mixed with the clear, clean smell of the soap, as suds mingled and flowed down her straight back. He could feel the bunched muscles beneath his hands, the result of a long day working on the boat. He knew those knots would be stiff and sore by morning. She would ache, but she'd never admit to him that she hurt.

He rubbed her back, under the pretense of scrubbing away imaginary dirt. That, and the hot shower, would go a long way toward easing her muscles. But he knew it wouldn't be enough.

Sara hummed deep in her throat as Matt rubbed and soaped. She let her head drop, her shoulders and neck exposed to his hands, asking without words for his touch. She stretched and turned, lifting her hands over her head. Taking his cue, Matt continued soaping her breasts, her belly, and lower.

Sara sighed once more as he ran the soapy sponge down each leg. "That feels good," she murmured. "I'll give you a week to stop."

Matt chuckled. "If we had a week, I'd take you up on that." He rinsed the sponge and put it back in the tray. "Maybe someday..." His voice trailed off, and he bent to plant a kiss on Sara's wet mouth. "My turn?" he asked.

Sara nodded. She reached for the bath brush, soaped it, and began rubbing it briskly over Matt's back. He stood still as she ran scratchy bristles across his body. Somehow it soothed his muscles, taking away the tension and fatigue that knotted his back and legs.

Chapter 3

Sara was staring at the ceiling, the first faint light of a summer morning outlining the windows, when the alarm buzzed. She had spent most of the night doing exactly that, staring and worrying. How had she ever talked herself into this? What in the hell had she been thinking?

She knew what she had been thinking. She had been thinking of the dwindling balance in their bank account and the cost of paying a hand. She had been desperate, and like all desperate people she had done some stupid things. And now she was stuck with the choices her stubborn pride had forced her to make.

Matt sat up, rubbing sleep from his eyes as he slapped at the alarm. "Damn thing," he muttered. He turned to Sara. She usually slept through his alarm, but this morning she was wide awake. She tried to smile.

"You okay?" he asked.

"Just nervous, I guess. You know how it is when you start a new job." She lifted the corners of her mouth, trying to hide her fear behind a smile.

"You'll be fine. There's nothing to worry about."

"Don't lie to me, Matt. There's plenty to worry about. What if I mess up?"

Matt looked hard at Sara. He was uneasy, even if he wouldn't admit it, and she knew it.

"Trust me. Just do what I tell you, when I tell you. If I say jump, don't stop to ask how high, just do it, and trust me to know why. Sort of like the Army, I guess. Pretend I'm the drill sergeant. Like in the movies." He grinned at her, taking some of the sting from his lecture. "And my first order is to give me a kiss."

"Sir." Sara fell into the game, and for a moment her smile felt genuine.

"Yes, sir."

• • •

Twenty minutes later, Matt parked the pickup in the dirt parking lot, two blocks up the hill from the boat docks of Newport, Oregon. He switched off the rattle of the ancient engine, and he and Sara climbed from the cab. The sky was dark, the gray of approaching storm clouds now hiding the light of dawn.

Neither one spoke as they walked down to the dock. His duffel bumped against his hip, and he could hear the gruff voices of the other crews. They called to each other, readying the boats for another fishing trip. Matt shivered inside his heavy coat and shoved his hands deeper in his pockets. Summer was here, but the Oregon coast was often cold in the morning. The chill had sunk deep in his bones, and he knew he wouldn't be warm again until he got back home. He could only hope that Sara realized what she had let herself in for.

"Is it always like this?"

"Like what?" He didn't want to answer her questions, didn't want to think about all the things she didn't know. She knew next to nothing about *Excelsior,* or about fishing. What made him think they could do this?

Matt glanced at her, hoping to reassure himself. She carried her duffel over her shoulder, leaning slightly against the unaccustomed weight, and worry lines bracketed her mouth. If she was going to survive this trip, he would have to be confident enough for both of them. And, he suspected, he would have to carry even more of the work than he usually did. He loved Sara, but he wished there was an experienced deck hand walking beside him down the wooden planks of the pier.

Lamp posts rose through the planking, the sulphurous yellow of vapor lights forming halos in the light rain that floated down from the gray skies. The planks were slick with rain, water puddling in cracks in the wood. At the base of the lampposts, starfish had been exposed by the receding tide. A young sea lion surfaced a few feet away, barking loudly, and gliding among the moored boats, drawn by the pungent odor of tons of baitfish sluicing into tanks.

The tide was coming back in now, climbing the pilings and slowly submerging the brilliant reds and oranges of the starfish. The boats were alive with crews preparing to cast off as the tide climbed over the breakwater. A flight of gulls wheeled overhead, screeching their demands for a handout. Ignored by the fishermen, they settled on the public pier a few hundred feet away, and dug at the trash left by vacationing tourists.

Matt and Sara passed the *Lois Jean,* and Matt heard someone call his name. He turned to see Josh waving from among the crab pots piled on the deck. When Matt let him go, Josh had taken a berth on the *Lois Jean,* and would be in the frigid waters of the Bering Sea for the next two or three months. "Good luck out there," Josh called.

Matt waved back and called, "You, too." Seeing Josh made Matt wish again that he was taking him, and not Sara. But Josh had to be paid, and Sara didn't, at least not in cash. He just hoped the cost of an inexperienced woman wasn't too high. There wasn't any margin for error in the middle of the Pacific.

• • •

Sara held the fuel nozzle in the starboard tank, the sharp odor of diesel assaulting her nose. She tried not to think about the pile of dollars the pale fluid represented. At least they weren't paying Josh to help, she was doing it.

When the pump shut off, she passed the hose to Matt, and he filled the port tanks. She stepped inside the wheelhouse, glancing at the mismatched electronic gear. Some of it had come with the boat, and some they bought second- and third-hand. It was obsolete, but it was what they had. And it was better than no instruments at all.

She pulled the checkbook from the cupboard where Matt kept his receipts. The cupboard door had broken, and was patched with an old piece of floor tile, brittle with age. A splinter of the tile scratched a narrow line of red across the back of her hand.

She tried not to look at the figures that represented their slim balance, as she wrote out the check for the fuel. Even so, she was depressingly aware that, without a catch, they wouldn't be able to pay their bills at the end of the month.

As they pulled away from the fuel dock, Sara didn't know what to do. She had no idea what her job was. Matt was doing everything all at the same time, everywhere on the entire thirty-seven foot length of the boat, and without a single wasted gesture. She felt useless, watching him wind the worn ropes and lash down the battered floats and dented buckets. Worse than useless, she could do something stupid, or dangerous, without even knowing it.

Although they had arrived after the others, Matt was first away from the dock, headed into the growing wind and rain, the steady thump of the diesel like a giant heartbeat echoing across the water.

Avoiding the lines and the controls, Sara shouldered the two duffels and carried them below. At least she knew where to stow their personal gear. As she clambered down the worn rungs of the narrow ladder to the tiny cabin that would be her home for the next few days, the boat heeled over and she heard Matt yell.

She dumped the bags on the floor and scrambled back up the ladder. If there was trouble, she would have to try and help Matt take care of it.

She found him standing at the wheel, his face drained of color, except for two harsh patches of red on his cheeks. His eyes were wide and she followed his stare. Just ahead of them, the stern of the *Janice Lee* threw up a sharp wake.

"What happened?"

"That stupid bastard!" Matt's voice shook with anger as he watched the *Janice Lee* churn toward the narrow mouth of the bay. "There's a no-wake speed limit in the harbor, and the sonofabitch knows it as well as I do." He breathed hard, and Sara watched as he battled his temper.

"I'm two minutes ahead of him at the fuel dock, and he has to make up the time by blowing by me, about ten knots over the limit." Matt shook his head. The anger drained from his voice, replaced by disgust. "Stupid bastard. Always looking for a shortcut. Moves like that get people killed."

Sara went back below to stow their gear. She stuffed clothes in the sticky drawers under the bench. She checked the meager assortment of cans in the dingy cupboard and thought about eating, but the close confines of the cabin and the fumes from the diesel soon combined to send her topside again. She didn't get seasick, but her empty stomach was having trouble adjusting to the steady motion. She told herself she just needed some fresh air.

Matt stood at the wheel, charts spread in front of him, one hand on the throttle control. He looked as though he was born at the helm of a ship. Though they were inside the harbor, the boat was rocking through a steady chop, part of it the wake of the speeding *Janice Lee*. As they approached the narrow mouth of the bay, the *Janice Lee* was clearing the breakwater, headed for the open sea with her throttle wide open.

The steep cliffs of the central Oregon coastline rose on either side of the bay, and salt spray erupted into the rain-soaked air with each wave that broke across the jagged rocks. It was a vivid reminder of the ocean's power.

A vein stood out on Matt's forehead, as he wrestled the wheel. The speeding boat had forced him to veer off course, and he had to pull his boat back into the narrow channel that formed a safe passage between the rocky outcroppings at the mouth of the bay. He was staring intently at the array of instruments in front of him as he guided *Excelsior* through the breakwater and into the open sea.

Sara poured a cup of coffee from the thermos and put it in the gimbaled holder that hung off the edge of the chart table. It fascinated her to watch the bearings hold the cup level and steady as the boat rocked along, riding the turbulent water.

Chapter 4

Rain hammered at the forward windows of the wheelhouse, and water ran along the side windows, driven sideways by the force of the wind. A narrow ribbon of water drops dotted one window where the caulking had chipped away. The rigging hummed with the wind, an eerie moaning sound that sent chills up Sara's spine.

"Couldn't we wait for this to pass?" she called to Matt, over the roar of the wind and rain.

"You know better than that. The season opens today, so we go today. Fish and Game can close it down if we reach the harvest limits, and I want to get as much as I can while it's open."

"But it's getting worse out there, Matt. Isn't there something — "

"We go when we have to." He cut her off, unwilling to debate what they both knew was a necessity. "This is a storm we can get through."

Sara retreated to a corner of the wheelhouse and stared out at the ocean. The radio crackled with static, then she heard the voice of the Coast Guard weather report. Although she didn't know the map coordinates, she understood enough to know the storm was coming up from the south.

She peered over Matt's shoulder at the compass. They were moving west by northwest, running on the ragged edge of the storm. She wondered how far they would have to go to escape the rain that pounded at the windows.

Looking back out the window, she watched as a wave broke across the deck. For a moment, the water stood a foot deep on the deck, then it began to run off through the scuppers. The water poured over the side in a steady stream, but before the deck was clear, another wave broke.

"Matt!" Sara's heart was racing as she watched the waves cover the deck.

"We can ride this out, Sara. It may take a couple hours, but it will pass. In the meantime, there isn't much else to do." He set his mouth in a grim line, his expression and body language dismissing Sara as completely as if she were still asleep in her bed at home.

Sara stood in the corner of the wheelhouse, uncertain whether to climb down the narrow ladder to the cabin, or stay where she was. Would it be worse to watch the storm batter them, or only hear it behind the closed curtains in the cabin? She decided to watch. Knowing was better.

The rain continued, a gray curtain obscuring the water ahead of them. The instruments glowed in the gloom of the dim light, and Matt continually glanced from the green and gold readouts to the charts spread across the table on his left.

The boat heeled hard to starboard, sending Sara into the starboard bulkhead with a thump that she knew would leave a bruise. For a moment she was pinned against the bulkhead, as though gravity was pulling her sideways. Instead, to her horror, it was pulling her down. They had caught a swell broadside and were listing heavily.

"Sonofabitch!" Matt's sharp curse grabbed her attention. She turned to look at him. He was braced against the rack holding the GPS system, hanging onto the wheel at an insane angle. His jaw was compressed with the strain of holding the wheel steady, and the muscles in his arms stood out in tense ropes.

Slowly, reluctantly, the boat began to right herself. Gravity loosened its hold on Sara, and she pried herself away from the bulkhead. She could feel the floor beneath her feet returning to a horizontal position, and she released the breath she didn't know she was holding.

Matt scrambled to get his feet back under him, and Sara watched in fascination as he dragged the wheel around. The boat turned into the swells, Matt's arms straining with the effort. Sara could feel it now, as they rode into and over the waves that were building.

They continued for long minutes, climbing laboriously up one wall of water after another, occasionally feeling the ocean give way beneath them as a wave crested and broke. *Excelsior* struggled through the wind and rain, plowing stubbornly ahead.

Sara clung to the edge of the chart table, her lips caught tight between her teeth. She had never been through a storm at sea, and she could only hang on as stubbornly as her husband and the boat, and hope they could ride it out. Matt continued to wrestle with the wheel, his entire concentration focused on the boat. Occasional drops of sweat ran down his face to drop, unheeded, from his chin. Sara suspected she could have exploded a bomb in the wheelhouse and he wouldn't have noticed, but he wasn't frightened or concerned, just determined.

After an hour that felt like a lifetime, Sara heard a change in the whistling in the lines. It dropped from a whine to a low moan, and she could feel the wind slowing. The rain continued, but the gray curtain thinned and she could see a short distance ahead.

The swells grew smaller, and now they were moving forward instead of climbing up and over mountains of water. As she watched him, the muscles in Matt's arms and back lost their rigidity, and she knew they were through the worst of it.

The diesel continued to throb and *Excelsior* plowed on through the rain. The deck was no longer awash, and Sara could see that the battered gear Matt had lashed down before leaving the dock was all in place.

The rain continued to fall through the morning, and Sara busied herself carrying coffee and sandwiches to Matt as he plowed ahead, scanning the water for signs of fish.

"Is there something else I can do?" she asked, breaking the relative silence that had followed the roar of the wind and the crashing waves. She had tried desperately to think of something, but she hesitated. It had begun to sink in that one stupid mistake could get them both killed. It was a sobering thought.

"Just be patient," he told her. "Once we find the fish, there will be plenty for you to do."

Chapter 5

Her question worried Matt, though he didn't tell her so. She would have to be told each move to make, and he wouldn't always have time to explain why. He hoped she would remember what he said, and do as he told her, without hesitating. He loved Sara, but he missed Josh. *Get over it,* he told himself. *We can't afford Josh.*

Despite her efforts to hide it, Matt had seen how Sara moved when she didn't think he was looking. She was stiff and sore from yesterday, and the pounding she had already taken was making it worse. He would have to watch her, make sure she didn't overdo and put herself completely out of commission, or make a mistake because she was tired. It was one more thing to worry about with her aboard.

Something in the water caught his eye, and he stared through the steady rain for a moment, then steered a course for the spot. After nearly ten years on the water, Matt knew what he was looking for. But as the catch declined, it was getting harder and harder to find.

"Fish?" Sara asked.

"Looks like it." Matt waved his hand in the general direction he was traveling, knowing Sara still couldn't see anything except empty miles of water. She wouldn't have to wait long, though.

Matt slowed the engines. He checked the charts again, and looked at the second-hand SONAR fish finder. They were over a popular feeding ground, and the SONAR was pinging like crazy. It was time to go to work.

Chapter 6

The engines were idling, the boat drifting for a moment. Matt pulled the hood of his jacket up and checked the zippers and belts. He pulled a pair of heavy deck boots over his shoes, then turned to help Sara into her gear.

Josh had taken his gear with him to the *Lois Jean,* and Sara had been outfitted with an odd lot of hand-me-downs and castoffs, most of them in sizes that would hold at least two of her. He pulled up the suspenders on her trousers, zipped them shut, and cinched them around the middle with an extra belt. Her jacket was a decent fit, and he tried to ignore the odd sensation he got as he fastened the crotch strap. Now wasn't the time.

Sara's boots were new. It had been their biggest expense, but Matt knew it was the one area where they couldn't risk any short-cuts. Her life might depend on staying on her feet, and a proper pair of boots could avert potential disasters.

He checked over her gear, and gave her a "thumbs up." She looked up at him, her tiny face dwarfed by the bulky jacket and over-hanging hood. She looked like a kid playing in dad's work clothes, and the thought gave Matt a chill. This wasn't play, it was real, it was dangerous, and his life was in her hands. *Please,* he prayed silently, *don't let her do some damn fool thing that'll get us both killed.*

"Let's go!" Matt signaled her to follow him to the stern where the giant spools containing the nets sat waiting.

He started the winch motors, engaged the clutch, and the nets began to unreel into the water. "Keep feeding them out," Matt called as he headed back to the helm.

• • •

This was it, the reason she had come. Sara clipped the safety line of her jacket to the jack line, as Matt had showed her. She adjusted the wrists of her gloves to make sure they were secure, and guided the nets coming off the spools.

Rain was still falling, hard and cold, and Sara was grateful for the foul-weather gear and thermal underwear. Without it she would have been soaked through, the minute she stepped out of the wheelhouse.

The spools turned at a steady rate, and Sara watched the heavy nets unrolling as Matt carefully maneuvered the boat to avoid tangling them. They spread across the water, disappearing beneath the surface, their position marked only by the bright orange floats that marked the edges of the net. Sara tried not to think about how much money floated in the wake of *Excelsior*. She concentrated, instead, on maintaining her footing on the wet, rolling deck.

Her hands grew chilled inside the bulky work gloves, but she knew better than to take the gloves off for even a minute. She had seen too many fishermen with mangled fingers from being caught in nets or tangled in lines. She wished she had thought to light the charcoal in her hand warmer, but it was too late now to stop and take care of it.

Sara concentrated on the nets as Matt piloted the boat through the choppy waters. The sky was getting darker, and a cold wind blew across the deck. Sara cinched her jacket tighter, and kept feeding out the net.

Her right arm was stiffening from the blow she had taken when they heeled over. All her muscles ached from yesterday's long hours readying the boat.

The wind changed direction, sending a volley of raindrops straight into her face. For a moment she couldn't see, but that didn't stop the nets. The spools turned and the net slid past her hands and over the transom into the ocean.

She swiped her face with one thick glove, dashing the water from her eyes, and focused on the nets.

Nothing else mattered for now, except laying the net in the water and pulling the fish out. She forced herself to ignore the protests of her arm each time she tugged at the heavy cable that formed the edge of the net. Her legs wobbled, and she locked her knees against the instant of weakness. She tried not to think, only to visualize the perfect placement of the net and the catch that would follow. Nothing else mattered. Just the net and the fish.

Sara's vision narrowed and she no longer saw the ocean, or the sky. She didn't feel the rain falling on her, or hear the drops as they hit the rubberized outer layer of her hood. The constant sound of the wind faded into the background as she listened to the creak of the spool and the whine of the winch. Her world contracted into a few square feet of deck, a width of transom, and the slow slide of the net through it.

The last section of net slithered over the transom, breaking the monotony of Sara's vision. The winch freewheeled, now relieved of its load. Remembering Matt's instructions, Sara quickly grabbed the motor control and shut it down. The sudden movement sent a spasm through her shoulder, and she gritted her teeth against the pain.

Sara allowed herself a few seconds" surrender to cold and fatigue, then she forced herself to clamber over the deck to the wheelhouse. The nets were in the water, but the day was far from over.

When she reached the wheelhouse, Matt handed her his coffee cup. The last of the coffee was only lukewarm. She swallowed, and felt the coffee all the way down. She had shared the sandwiches earlier that morning, but that was a long time ago.

A sigh escaped her lips, and Matt gave her a sharp glance.

"Tired?"

"A little," she admitted. "But I know there's a lot more to do." Matt reached for her and draped a rubber-clad arm over her dripping shoulders. "There's time for a quick break," he said. "I'd really appreciate if you made some hot coffee. Just wait for it, and bring me a fresh cup, if you would."

Sara pulled off her boots and clambered out of her jacket and fishing pants. She left them hanging in the wheelhouse. Getting them back on would be painful, but she couldn't climb the ladder in them.

When she reached the bottom, she started a pot of coffee, and gingerly lowered herself to the narrow bench that was the cabin's only seating. It was cold and hard, but being able to sit at all was a slice of heaven. Especially since she knew another session of hell was waiting for her topside.

Hell, Sara decided, wasn't fire and brimstone. It was cold, dark rain falling everywhere, soaking into everything. While she waited for the coffee, she stripped off her shoes and socks. Even though her boots were watertight, she had managed to get some water in her shoes, and her socks were damp.

With an effort, she levered herself off the bench and reached in the drawer underneath for a clean pair of socks. The feel of soft, dry cotton on her cold feet was a pleasant shock. She sat for a minute, letting her feet warm, but the chill didn't leave. Sighing, she dug in the drawer and pulled out a second pair. At this rate she would be out of dry socks by tomorrow afternoon.

That would be a problem for tomorrow. For today, she had to get back on deck. She clutched the metal vacuum bottle in her hand and began the crawl up the ladder to the wheelhouse.

By the time she reached the third rung of the ladder, Sara's arms were shaking in protest. Her muscles spasmed, and she longed for a few minutes to rest. Instead, she hooked an arm through the rung in front of her and hung on until the tremor passed, then continued up the ladder. There was no time to rest. Not now.

When she crawled back into the wheelhouse, Matt took the coffee and quickly filled his cup. Blowing across the surface to cool it, he wrapped one hand around the mug. After a moment, he changed hands. Sara understood what he was doing, using the hot coffee to warm his hands. She had done the same thing just a minute earlier as she filled the vacuum bottle.

Static filled the wheelhouse, as the radio crackled to life.

"*Excelsior. Excelsior.* This is the vessel *Lois Jean.*"

Matt picked up the mike and keyed the switch. "*Lois Jean,* this is *Excelsior.* Switch and answer on channel six eight, over."

Matt switched the radio from the hailing frequency, and Sara heard Josh's voice through the tinny speaker of the radio. "We thought you might be out here. Passed three boats with their nets out about five miles south of you. Looks like we might have more weather coming in. Over."

"Roger that. As though we didn't have enough already. Have a safe trip. Over."

"We're careful." Josh's voice turned anxious for a moment. "Any idea what was up with the *Janice Lee* this morning? Looked like he almost swamped you before you could get out of his way."

"Don't know, but he was sure in a hurry. When I get back, I'll talk to the harbormaster about the speeding."

"Do that. Give that pretty deckhand a hug for me. We'll see you in a couple months. Out." The voice dropped out, replaced by the quiet hum of background noise, and Matt switched back to the hailing and emergency channel.

Sara struggled into her gear, managing to dress herself without Matt's help. While she buckled and zipped and cinched, he maneuvered the boat into position to haul in the nets. By the time she was finished, he was locking the autopilot.

"I'll need your help for a couple minutes, then I want you to come up here and take the wheel." Matt flipped up his hood, and his face faded into shadow.

"The wheel? I can haul nets." Sara tried to make her voice convincing. She was determined to do her share.

"We take turns. That's how I do it with Josh, that's how I'll do it with you."

"But the autopilot - "

"I don't trust the autopilot for long, and neither should you. Like I said this morning, just do what I tell you, and we'll do fine." Matt's voice rose, and Sara could hear the edge of command that he'd learned as a crew leader on other boats. "It may sound silly to you, but I'm the captain on this vessel, and my word is the law.

"And don't argue. You're tired, and tired people make mistakes. Out here a mistake can get us both real dead, real fast. And dead is forever." He turned and opened the hatch, admitting a blast of cold rain, carried on the rising wind.

His words stung, as though she had been slapped, but she knew he was right. She cinched her jacket tight, and followed him to the stern.

The wind pulled Matt's words away, and she had to depend on his hand signals for direction. They pulled up the rough edge of the net and secured it to the spool. She helped him open the hatch covers to receive the fish, and to start the winch motor.

Matt checked the motor setting, and gave her a "thumbs up." "You go forward," he yelled over a lull in the wind. "Keep the compass steady and the engines at slow. Just hold her on course while I haul in the nets." He kissed her hurriedly, and shoved her toward the helm. "Go! I'll handle this."

Her hands shook as Sara took the wheel. She had piloted the boat before, for brief minutes when they were docking, or helping Matt when he 'test drove' *Excelsior* after repairs. But she had never had the wheel on the open water, and never during a storm.

Gripping the wheel tightly with both hands, Sara focused on the compass. She couldn't worry about Matt hauling in the nets by himself, or wonder if they had managed to get any fish. She stared at the compass and willed it to stay at the same heading. If she just concentrated hard enough, she could keep the course.

Chapter 7

Matt struggled with the heavy nets and the rising wind. It was a tough job, and it was even harder without a hand. But he and Josh had done it, and he was determined to make this work with Sara. He could feel the boat wallowing a little as the seas rose, but she seemed to be holding the course he had set. His job now was to trust Sara and get the nets in before the weather worsened.

The winches strained, pulling the water-heavy nets from the ocean. A few black rockfish fell from the nets, eventually growing to a steady stream. It wasn't a full load by any measure, but it was better than he had expected.

They would need at least another load this size to make this trip pay, he thought as he watched the fish slide into the hold. But right now he needed to relieve Sara. She was too exhausted to stay at the wheel for long. He slammed the hatch shut, tightened the latch, and made his way to the helm.

Sara was staring at the compass, her hands tight on the wheel, white knuckles straining to hold it steady. Matt could see the tight line of her jaw jutting from the hood of her jacket, the muscles at the corners bunched with tension. Her shoulders were hunched, the muscles tensed into knots that he could feel without seeing them.

When he touched her shoulder she jumped as though she had been scalded. She had been so focused on her course that she hadn't heard him come in. Matt stroked her arm, unwinding her fingers one at a time from the wheel.

"Thanks, honey. You did a good job."

Sara surrendered the wheel to Matt, and retreated to her corner of the wheelhouse. He heard her peel off her gear and hang it on the hook by the hatch. She moved slowly, and he wondered how long it would be before she gave in to exhaustion.

The wind and rain battered their little boat for another hour before it relented. Usually he and Josh would trade off, but this time it was up to Matt. He wrestled the wheel, feeling the muscles in his arms and shoulders straining to hold a steady course.

He continued north, trying to stay ahead of the main body of the storm. Finally, the wind died and the rain slacked off. The western sky was light and Matt could see the dark clouds rolling eastward, headed for the shoreline. The coastal cities were in for a rainy night.

Sara had been quiet for a long time, but he'd been too busy to notice. Now he turned, and found her curled up in the corner, her head pillowed on her arm, sound asleep. He set the autopilot and, although it wasn't fully dark, started making the boat fast for the night.

He made a cursory examination of the deck, and cast a quick glance over the nets, checking for damage. Nothing to worry about. A little water here and there, but no lines had snagged, no nets had ripped.

He took a minute to check the hold. It was about a third full. A better catch than he had expected. If Josh were here, they'd spread the nets again and go on. But Sara was exhausted, and they had done as much as they could for one day.

Matt wanted to run north another hour or so, to put them well out of the weather for the night. But he couldn't leave Sara asleep on the deck. He put one hand on her shoulder and shook her gently. Pain flashed across her sleeping face at the touch, and Matt yanked his hand back. He hadn't meant to hurt her.

Sara's eyes blinked open, and she looked up blearily at Matt. "Are we there yet?"

Matt laughed out loud, partly in amusement and partly in relief. At least her sense of humor had survived their first day, even if her body had given out. There was hope for tomorrow. "You're as there as you're gonna get today," he said. "I'm thinking it's time to call it quits. Go below. Get warm. Get some rest. I'll be down in a little while."

Chapter 8

"You better eat your ice cream, before it melts," Sara said. She reached for the scoop and the carton, sliding them across the postage stamp table in front of Matt. The bench was hard and narrow, but it felt good to rest her battered body. It also felt good to have Matt's arm around her, and she wondered what it would be like to make love with the constant rocking of the boat.

Matt had heated a can of stew and they had eaten quickly, hunger battling with exhaustion. Now they were sharing the carton of vanilla ice cream Sara had smuggled on board hidden in the grocery bag. It was one of Matt's favorite things, but she didn't think it would keep.

"In fact," she continued talking around a spoonful, "I was worried it wouldn't last this long."

Matt shook his head. "Honey, there's four tons of ice down there. I think the ice cream was safe for a few hours."

• • •

A tendril of worry snaked through his brain. Sara knew so little about the workings of the boat. So many things could go wrong.

He wrenched his thoughts from the dark images that were forming. Certainly things could go wrong, but he was an experienced seaman, and he would just have to see that she didn't make any major mistakes.

Outside, the night was pitch black. They were drifting, alone on the ocean. The other boats were still south of him, strung out in a miles-long picket line to drift with the currents and the wind through the night.

But inside there was light from the electric bulb powered by the generator, and the hatches were battened down against the cold night wind. He buried his face in Sara's dark hair and planted an affectionate kiss on the top of her head.

"I can't eat all this, you know," Matt said, gesturing at the half-empty carton. "It will keep 'til tomorrow. Really," he said, at Sara's skeptical look. "Believe me, that much ice will give us plenty of chill to keep half a carton of ice cream for one day." He picked up the carton and bumped his hip against Sara's to scoot her over and let him out. As he went up the ladder to the deck, he called back to her. "Remember, I depend on that ice to keep hundreds of pounds of fish fresh. A little ice cream isn't even a challenge."

• • •

"Wow." Matt's voice floated down from the wheelhouse, and the tone of awe drew Sara up the ladder and out the door. The thought occurred to her that it probably wasn't called a door, and she wondered what was the right name. But the moment she stepped through onto the deck she stopped thinking about what to call the door. She stopped thinking, stopped breathing, for long seconds.

Stars. The word was inadequate for the spectacle that spread across the heavens and stretched from horizon to horizon. She had never in all her life seen stars like the ones she was looking at this minute. Stars so thick that they looked like a giant flowing cloud. She knew the Milky Way, had seen it clearly on moonless nights on the beach, or in the mountains. But she had never seen it like this. It made her feel the same awe she had heard in Matt's voice.

Matt secured the hatch, and they stood for a few moments, staring at the deep black of the night sky. Sara could tell where east was because the lights of the cities lining the coast glowed faintly against the black of the night. She shivered, and wished she'd worn a sweater when she stepped out on deck.

"Cold?" Matt asked. He peeled off his light jacket and hung it over her shoulders. "We probably ought to go in. The sun comes up early and we'll be up with it."

Sara nodded, and they turned back to the cabin. "Is it always like this?" she asked. Her voice was low, hardly more than a whisper. It was as if talking out loud would disturb the distant stars.

Chapter 9

Making up the bunk reminded Sara of camping trips as a kid. She remembered putting her bedroll on the shelf of the camper that stuck out over the top of the truck cab. When she was eight, it was a treat. Now she and Matt were going to sleep in a space not much bigger, under the deck and over the hold.

She was tired and her entire body ached. Her right shoulder, the one Matt had touched when he woke her up, hurt each time she moved. She suspected it was one big bruise, but she hadn't looked at it yet.

"I miss my shower already," she muttered.

"I know. You'll get used to it." There was no sympathy in Matt's pronouncement, just a statement of fact.

She turned back to give him a guilty look. She hadn't meant for him to hear her, but the boat was smaller than she realized, the quarters a little slice of space grudgingly carved from the working area. Matt looked as tired as she was, and she knew he had done a lot more of the work. She wasn't being fair.

"Actually, since you're the one who will have to smell me when I haven't had a proper bath, you're the one who had better get used to it." She grinned at him, and went back to fussing with the bed.

• • •

Matt watched Sara's bottom wiggle as she crawled and stretched across the bunk. There wasn't a lot of headroom, but she was being extremely cautious, and she kept waving her backside in the cutest way. Not that now would be a good time to tell her that.

"It's not that bad," he said. "You just close the door to the head, pull the curtains if there's anybody around, and turn on the water. Turn the water off while you wash, then turn it back on to rinse. You'll be clean enough."

"Clean enough for what?"

"Clean enough for me." This time Matt couldn't keep the leer out of his voice. His reward was a tired grin, and an extra wiggle.

"In here?"

"Well, we could go out on deck, but there's a bit of wind tonight, and it might get a little cold."

"In your dreams, buddy." Sara wasn't about to admit she had actually been thinking the exact same thing just a few minutes earlier. She was tired and sore, but tempted. Even if the spirit was willing, maybe even eager, she didn't know if the flesh would cooperate.

The shower resembled a travel trailer bathroom, with a hand-held shower hanging on the wall, and the entire closet-sized room was the shower stall. There was no way they could repeat their water play of the previous evening, since the two of them could not fit in the room at the same time. So much for that fantasy.

Sara sprayed herself quickly and shut off the water. She soaped carefully and rinsed hurriedly under a trickle of luke-warm water. To conserve fuel, Matt had installed a solar heater for bath water. Still, she had no idea how much hot water there was, and she didn't think there had been enough sun to heat it up anyway.

She toweled dry, but she still felt cold and clammy. One day at sea and she was lusting after a full spray of hot water. She reminded herself that it was only for a few days, and concentrated on what was at stake. Only their entire livelihood and their future. By comparison, this was a minor annoyance, one she could live with.

When she stepped out into the cabin, Matt had transformed it somehow in the few minutes she was gone. The table where they had eaten was folded against the wall, and a thin cushion topped the bench, making it a more inviting place to sit.

He'd shut off the harsh overhead bulb, and instead the cabin was lit with the dim glow of battery-powered night lights. The effect was to soften all the edges, and hide the nicks and scratches that scarred the woodwork. The bed was nothing more than a shadowy cave above the back of the bench, its cramped space disguised in the dark.

Matt had changed, too. His jeans and jacket were hung by the door, ready for morning, and he had wrapped himself in his plaid flannel robe while he waited his turn in the closet-sized shower. He stood up from the bench when she came out of the shower, and gave her a quick hug as they squeezed past each other to trade places.

"You smell just fine," he said, the stubble of his beard scratching her soft cheek. When she flinched at the scraping, he looked chagrined. "Guess I'll have to start shaving out here. Never bothered when I was out with Josh."

Sara smiled up at him through her long eyelashes and winked slowly. "I bet Josh never worried about how he smelled, either."

"You know, I do believe you're right." Matt squeezed her bottom, then released her. "Don't go away. I'll be right back."

Sara could hear the short bursts of water as Matt showered. She could imagine how he would look, the hard ropes of muscle in his arms and legs contrasting with the solid slabs of chest and back, and his firm round backside. Even after five years of marriage, it was a sight that stopped her heart every time. She hoped it would always be that way. They just had to get through this trip. Well, maybe a few trips. She knew she could be tough. If she didn't make a stupid mistake, they would make it.

Matt's damp head peeked around the shower door, the small cloud of steam hidden in the dim light. "Still there?"

"No, I went for a moonlight stroll. I'll be back in an hour or two."

Matt rolled his eyes and stepped into the cabin, wearing nothing but a big smile. Sara enjoyed the view, but the thought crossed her mind that he ought to be freezing. She was wearing flannel pajamas and two pair of socks, and she still felt cold, while Matt seemed quite comfortable in nothing but his birthday suit and a smile. It certainly improved the scenery in the dimly lit cabin.

"Hi there, handsome. What are you up to?"

Matt winked, and sat next to her. "Nothing. Yet. You have something in mind?" He draped an arm over her shoulder and his hand snaked down to fondle her breast for an instant, then retreat.

"Nooo.—" She drew out the word into three syllables. " — Nothing special. But I figured it was probably getting toward bed time." She snuggled against him and sighed. "And to tell the truth, I am freezing. How come you look so comfortable?"

"I'm used to it, I guess." He shrugged. "And a hot shower always helps, even if it is short."

"Hot?! How did you get a hot shower? It was barely warm when I was in there."

"Did you set the mixture for the solar tank and the cold tank?"

"What mixture? I turned on the faucet, it was warm, so I figured that was as good as it gets."

Matt hung his head, and tried to look sheepish, but a grin tugged at the corners of his mouth. "Oh, honey," he gave in to the chuckle he'd been fighting, and reached for Sara. "I am so sorry. I thought you knew how to work the controls. Tomorrow, I promise, you get as much hot water as you need."

Sara sat completely still for a minute. She would never learn all the things she had to know. The shower didn't matter, but what other mistakes, dangerous ones, might she make?

Matt looked down at her. "We probably ought to get to bed. The sun comes up awfully early out here. You want the front or the back?"

Sara considered the question. She might feel trapped in the back, but Matt always needed to get up in the middle of the night, and he would have to crawl over her. Then again, there were times that might be kind of fun.

"Back, I guess. That way you can get up without me being in the way. That okay with you?"

Matt nodded, and shifted on the bench to let her climb up into the bunk. It took her a few minutes to get turned around and under the blankets, while Matt waited on the bench below.

"You okay up there?"

"I think so. It's a little awkward, getting in here, but I think I'm settled. You coming up?"

"In a sec. I need to check the hatch and turn out the lights." With his robe draped over his shoulders, Matt shuffled the few feet to the door, and checked it. He checked the water faucets in the head, and tapped the battery lights off.

A single, dim battery light glowed on the wall above the bench. It provided enough light to move around, if one was careful. Matt tapped it out, and hoisted himself into the bunk. He didn't need the light. He knew *Excelsior* better than he knew their apartment.

Chapter 10

Sara was still bundled up in her flannel pajamas and heavy socks, but she began to warm up when Matt crawled in with her. Burrowing into the covers, she managed to stop shivering and slip off her socks. It seemed so silly to be lying there with heavy pajamas when Matt was naked.

She was warmer now, the blankets trapping the heat of two healthy, young bodies. She skinned down the pajama bottoms, and felt more comfortable and relaxed. It was silly, really, to be dressed when Matt would keep her warm.

Matt's arm went around Sara and pulled her close, but not tight. It was friendly enough, but Sara didn't feel any desire in his embrace, just a friendly arm. A little stab of disappointment went through her. Maybe she should give him some encouragement.

Sara rolled over and reached her arm around Matt. Excited by her own daring, she ran a fingertip along his ear lobe, and down the smooth line of his cheek. Even in the dark she could picture his face, the strong line of his jaw, his dark eyes, the little bump on his nose where he'd broken it playing football in high school. She had looked at that face every day since the second grade, and had known even then that she loved him.

She snuggled closer to him, and rested her head against his chest. His skin was warm, and she heard a tiny catch in his breathing. He was getting the message.

She slid her arm down his side, her fingers trailing along the ticklish skin under his arm. She rolled, and hissed as pain shot through her bruised shoulder.

"You okay?" Matt's whisper was loud in the silence of the cabin.

"Just a bruise." Wiggling against Matt, she took some of the pressure off the bruise, but it was a reminder of the abuse her body had taken. *Maybe this wasn't such a great idea.*

"Do you want me to stop?" Matt ran his hand over her hip, and up her side, to hold her face in the dark. She could feel him hard against her thigh, and she knew he didn't want to stop. Neither did she, despite the pain in her shoulder and the ache of her muscles.

"No."

The calluses of his palm rubbed her cheek as he tilted her head and brought his mouth down over hers.

The feel of his lips, the velvety softness of his mouth on hers, was a sharp contrast to the roughness of his work-toughened hands. His mouth reminded her of the tender young boy she had fallen in love with, but his hands were the hard-working man she married.

"No," she repeated.

She twisted her fingers in Matt's hair, pulling his mouth hard against hers. She nibbled his lower lip, and felt his response against her bare leg. His reaction fed her own, and she could feel the tingling, warming sensation growing inside her. Tired though she was, Matt's kisses and the press of his body excited her.

She pressed herself tight to Matt's body, ignoring the protest of her aching muscles. She wanted him, wanted to feel his mouth and his hands on her body, touching all the sensitive spots that pulsed with need.

She pulled her mouth from Matt's and slid her tongue over his lips, teasing and licking. Her teeth tugged at his lips and nipped his tongue as it reached for hers. She touched his face in the dark, running her fingers along the arch of his eyebrow, the ridge of his cheekbone and down his jaw.

Her hand trailed down, resting flat on his chest, and her mouth followed, burrowing into his neck. She licked the hollow of his neck and felt the groan, deep in his throat, against her mouth. He didn't move, waiting for her to continue, but she could feel the hunger and need in his embrace, as he crushed her to him.

Matt pressed against Sara in the narrow bunk, his arms tightened around her. She brushed her palm against his nipple and slid her legs along his. She felt brave, testing her growing self-confidence. She could hardly believe she was doing this, and her body was demanding that she hurry. But she could hurt herself if she wasn't careful.

"Are you sure?" Matt whispered. His concern was touching, but her answer was a swift pinch of one nipple.

He cupped one hand under her chin and raised her face to his. In the dark she couldn't see him, but she could feel the heat of his skin, hear his ragged breathing, smell the faint trace of toothpaste and soap as he covered her mouth with a deep, demanding kiss.

She was still dressed in the long flannel pajama top. The buttons at her throat were undone, and Matt slid his hand around her neck to rest below her ear. He held her there, cradling her head in his hand while he kissed her, his thumb rubbing along her jaw and under her chin.

Sara's hand remained still on Matt's chest, and she moved her other one next to it. A groan welled up from deep inside Matt, and he pushed against her hands. She could feel his need building. He wanted her to touch him, to pinch and stroke and squeeze every part of him.

Still holding her mouth with his, Matt worked the buttons open on Sara's top. As each button opened, she felt his fingers on her bare skin, first on the soft swell of her breasts, then the solid muscles that covered her ribs, and the soft curve of her belly. When he released the last button, he reached the soft thatch between her legs, growing damp with her excitement.

He laid his hand on her, resting it on the springy curls.

"Oh, yes," she breathed. She could feel a faint pulse, the echo of her hammering heart, in the swelling lips. Her hips rose off the mattress, pressing into his palm. His fingers curled, one sliding along the slick wetness and for an instant he touched her hard clitoris.

She gasped, then exhaled in a low moan. He withdrew his hand, running it along her side to reach her breast. Sara's hands teased his hard nipples, and he returned the attention.

"You like that?" Matt asked. Sara answered with a groan. She could feel the sensitive skin of her nipple harden in his fingers.

She pressed her body tight to his and arched her back, pushing her breast into his hand.

He lowered his mouth to her breast, tasting her sweet skin. He licked her hard nipple, then blew gently across it. It drove her wild, sending pleasure through her. His mouth moved lower, but the cramped space of the bunk wouldn't allow him to move far, and he quickly returned to suck at her nipple.

"Little cramped, isn't it?" Sara's voice was ragged with desire.

"We'll manage," Matt answered, flicking his tongue across first one nipple and then the other.

Her hands were roaming across his body now. She held his head to her breast for a moment, then resumed her exploration. She ran her fingernails across his stomach, around his belly button, then along the line of hair that led lower.

"Touch me!" he demanded, sliding his body back toward the top of the bed. Her hand closed around his shaft, and he pushed himself into her fingers, groaning with pleasure. "Yes. Harder." She squeezed, and he leaped in her hand.

He reached between her legs, his fingers searching for the warm, wet place he had found earlier. He slid a finger along the cleft, and he probed between her lips.

He rubbed his fingers slowly along the narrow slit, wet with her juices. His fingers found her clitoris, and Sara bucked and gasped.

"There," she said, her voice low and harsh. "Oh, yes. Right there."

Matt's fingers moved slowly, making tiny circles. Sara wanted to push herself onto his hand, to drive herself to the point of no return, but she waited. She held her hips still, savoring the sweet pleasure and the building excitement.

Her hands were on Matt's erection, rubbing, squeezing, teasing. She ran her fingers down the length of him, around the base, and back to the sensitive tip. He was alive in her hand, rock hard and quivering with his need. They were both on the edge.

"Make love to me," she whispered against his ear. She rained kisses along his jaw line and found his mouth with hers. His kiss was full of his hunger and need, answering her need. She rolled away, opening herself for him.

The bunk was too low for Matt to move on top of her, and for a moment frustration washed over her. There wasn't enough room to move, and she wanted him, deeply, desperately. Wanted to hold him deep inside her and feel him move in her.

Impatient, she rolled against him, laying her leg over his body, and pulling him close. He moved in response, his penis hard against her soft lips. His need pushed him closer, until he slid inside her.

Sara wrapped her leg tight around Matt's waist, pulling him deep into her. He filled her, and she felt as though every nerve in her body was concentrated in the channel that held him, sending intense pleasure throughout her body.

Matt reached around her, cupping her bottom in his strong hands, squeezing her cheeks and forcing himself deeper inside her. They lie still for a moment, bodies crushed together, teetering on the edge of abandon.

"Now," Sara breathed. "Please, now." She was almost begging, consumed with need.

"Now," Matt answered. He pulled back, sending waves of longing through her, then plunged back into her. Sara bucked against him, taking the hard length of him deep inside.

She couldn't stop now, couldn't wait any longer. Matt began to move, and she answered his thrusts with her own, matching his rhythm. She rocked against him as he slid deep inside her, knowing the end was near. He thrust again, his hands clutching her ass, and she pushed hard, grinding against him.

Her head fell back, her back arched, and Sara gave a cry of completion. Pleasure flashed over her, knotting her straining muscles.

"Yes, baby. Let it go. That's it." She could hear Matt urging her on, encouraging her to surrender, as she fell over the top and began the long slow slide down the other side.

Matt was pushing hard now, his hips slamming into her, his hands gripping her ass. He gasped, driving himself deep inside her. He groaned and bucked, calling her name. He trembled with the force of his climax, his hips continuing to pump against her. He moaned as his movements slowed, and his grip relaxed.

Sara turned her face and met Matt's mouth. His kiss was soft, his hunger spent in her body. He held her close, resting her head on his chest, and nuzzling her hair.

"You okay?" he asked.

"Very okay," she murmured. "But you knew that, didn't you?"

"You were awfully tired," he said. "I was afraid I might hurt you."

Sara chuckled deep in her throat. "I was a little afraid myself, but I was curious what it would be like on the boat." She was glad it was dark, so Matt wouldn't see the blush climbing her cheeks.

"Were you now?" Matt's voice was drowsy, his tone light and teasing. "And how was it?"

Now Sara was really blushing, her courage spent, but the intense darkness hid her, and she answered his question. "Well, I'd say pretty good, wouldn't you? But I didn't notice the boat much."

"Well, it was new to me, too. But now that you mention it, I didn't notice much about the boat, either." He bent to plant a light kiss on her lips. "I wonder why that might be?"

Matt's voice had grown fainter, and Sara knew he was close to sleep. She sighed and settled against Matt's side. The rocking of the boat as it drifted with the currents was odd, but as she sank into the rhythm of the motion, she began to drift herself. Her eyes closed, and soon she was asleep.

• • •

The bed shifted, and Sara's sleep-fogged brain told her it was Matt, getting out of bed for another day of work. He always left so early, and he tried hard not to wake her though he often did. But this time, instead of leaning down to kiss her goodbye, Matt continued to snore.

Something was wrong. Sara opened her eyes expecting the faint light of early morning. But she could see nothing. It was pitch black, she could hear Matt's soft snores next to her, and the bed continued to pitch and roll.

Disoriented and confused, panic shot through Sara. What woke her up? A noise? Was someone in the apartment? She buttoned her pajama top with trembling fingers and tried to remember where she'd left her robe. Her heart raced and her breath caught in her chest. Why didn't Matt wake up?

As she tried to swing her feet over the side of the bed, she ran her toe into something solid. The pain in her toe cleared the last of the cobwebs from her brain, and she remembered where she was. She was on *Excelsior*, in the middle of the ocean. Her eyes were adjusting to the darkness, and she could make out the sleeping form of her husband between her and the opening of the bunk, barely discernable as a shade lighter than the darkness that surrounded her.

Panic subsided, replaced by the fear and dread she had carried all day. She couldn't even sleep through the night without waking up in a panic. How could she expect to get through the entire trip?

She reached one arm out, feeling for something solid in the rolling mass of the bed. Her arm fell across Matt's back, and he sighed in his sleep and rolled over. His arm went around her, his leg over hers, and he buried his face against her shoulder. Within seconds, his quiet snores filled the cabin again.

If Matt could sleep through whatever had awakened her, she shouldn't worry. She drew comfort from his solid warmth, and thought back over the day. She had ridden out the storm, and laid the nets. She had taken the helm while Matt hauled in the nets, and she had kept going when she had to.

And, she remembered with a rush of warmth, she had initiated their lovemaking. She could do lots of things.

And if she could do it today, she could do it again tomorrow. She held onto that thought for reassurance and let her exhaustion drag her back down into a deep sleep.

Chapter 11

When the first light of dawn pricked Matt's eyes, he refused to open them, and snuggled closer to Sara. It felt good to hold her, to feel her bare legs against his, to pull her close to him. She fit so well along the length of him, her sweet, round, little bottom nestled against his crotch.

Matt could feel the first stirrings of desire, and he pulled Sara tight to him. She was warm and soft, still asleep, her breathing deep and quiet. He felt a pleasant, familiar heaviness in his penis.

Matt rested his hand flat on her ribcage, teasing himself with the thought of the soft, round breasts that he could almost feel along the edge of his hand. He would only have to move a fraction of an inch to nudge the heavy curve of the underside of her breast. It was one of the delights of being home, the opportunity to make sweet morning love with his wife.

The sharp slap of a small wave against the hull of the boat made Matt aware of where he was, and destroyed the fantasy he had been building. He felt the letdown of reality throughout his body, his hand falling limp against Sara's flannel pajama top. Matt dragged himself from the bunk to the head.

Dawn was lighting the cabin, and he knew further sleep was impossible. He fumbled into his clothes, hoping he could avoid waking Sara. She looked so small and vulnerable, her face soft and round, her hair loose on the pillow. She shouldn't have to be here, he thought guiltily as he started water for coffee. The least he could do was allow her to escape into her dreams for a little longer.

The smell of coffee, though, seemed to reach into Sara's sleep, and to draw her out of her dreams. She sat up on her elbows, rubbing the sleep from her eyes, and trying to focus on Matt.

"Is that coffee?"

"It's what passes for it out here." Matt poured a mug half full and carried it to the bunk. "Careful, it's hot," he said as he handed it up to her.

"Hold on." Sara handed the cup back, and slid her legs over the side of the bunk. Her pajama top was rumpled, her bare legs hanging over the edge of the bunk, her hair still mussed from her pillow. She was about the sexiest thing Matt had ever seen. Maybe the fish could wait, just this once.

Sara reached for the coffee, and it sloshed a few drops on Matt's hand. The heat stung, and he turned to the sink to run cold water over the spot. It reddened, but didn't blister.

"Oh, honey! I'm sorry." Sara slid down from the bunk, her top riding up as she did, providing a view that succeeded in distracting Matt from the mild burn on his hand.

"No harm done," he assured her, his head filled with images of her legs stretching for the floor and the wrinkled flannel riding up her thighs.

He didn't add that he had worked with much worse, like the rope burn that had scarred his palm two years earlier. His own damned fault for not wearing his gloves, and it left him with a reminder of what happened when he got careless. She was used to him coming home injured, and she knew about the scar, but he'd never told how careless he had been.

Sara yawned and stretched, rolling her shoulders and neck, wincing as the sore muscles pulled and stretched. She reminded Matt of a cat when she moved like that, as though there were no real bones in her body. The fish would wait, he decided. But Sara snatched up her clothes from the cubbyhole where they were stowed, and stepped into underwear and jeans.

Matt swallowed hard. They were out here to work. He had considered a lot of potential problems for this trip, but he hadn't counted on Sara being such a distraction. He didn't know why, but it was much worse than at home. He took his coffee and went up to the wheelhouse.

The sun was still below the horizon, the sky light, but overcast. Time to go to work. It took him a few minutes to warm up the engines and check the charts. Though the GPS was old, it gave him accurate readings. He didn't even need the charts, but it reassured him to confirm the readings. His dad and uncles had taught him to read a chart before he was old enough to shave, and he prided himself on his ability to navigate by the stars.

By the time he climbed back down to the cabin, Sara had made the bed and folded down the table. She had fresh coffee brewing, and ham slices sizzling in a frying pan.

"Wow! Josh never cooked breakfast." And Josh never looked like that in a pair of jeans, either. Ham wasn't going to satisfy all his hungers.

Sara's smile was a little strained, and there were dark smudges under her eyes. Matt guessed she hadn't slept well her first night aboard. He tried to remember his first night on the water, but he couldn't. It seemed like he had always been out on the ocean, as far back as he could recall.

He sat at the table, savoring the few minutes of peace before they started work for the day.

Chapter 12

When Sara finished cleaning up after breakfast, she started up the ladder to the wheelhouse. Matt stood at the helm, one hand on the wheel, his coffee in the other. The thought came, as it did each time she caught sight of him in that pose, that Matt belonged on *Excelsior*. He was at home here, the place he was born to be.

She climbed the remaining rungs to the helm, and slipped her arms around Matt's waist. "Mmmmm. You feel good."

Matt stuck his coffee in the holder and snaked an arm around her, pulling her up next to him. "So do you, sweetheart. What are you up to?"

"Just came to see how you're doing. Quiet this morning."

"So far, but I'm feeling lucky."

"Are you now?" Sara's throaty reply made Matt realize the unintended double meaning.

"Don't I wish!" He kissed her. "But, no, I mean I think we'll find some more fish. In fact -" Matt withdrew his arm and changed course.

Sara swallowed hard and reached for her gear. The seas were rising again and the sky was overcast. The day promised to be another stormy one, and she was starting out sore and tired. This time she knew what lay ahead, and she was determined to hold up her end of the bargain.

She waited at the stern for Matt to give her the signal, and began the laborious process of spreading the nets. The winch turned the spool at a steady rate, and she guided the nets into the choppy water.

Sara wished they could ride out the rain in the cabin, where they could be relatively warm and dry. She understood what Matt had told her. After years of living on the coast she knew that the season could be closed at any minute, cutting off their income. They had to fish when they could, and the weather be damned.

The rain drove at her, obscuring her vision. There were small white caps all around the boat, and they were beginning to rock in the rough seas. With each pitch, her legs struggled to maintain her balance, and she felt the strain and pull of overworked muscles with every movement.

Inside the bulky gloves, her hands were warmed by the smoldering charcoal in the hand warmers. She was glad she had remembered to light it. Without the added warmth she was afraid her hands would cramp and refuse to grip the heavy lines. Even with the constant heat, fatigue was weakening her grip.

The boat rose up the face of a swell and plowed down the back side, jerking Sara off her feet and slamming her into the spool. The spool turned, pushing her toward the stern where the nets continued their relentless slide into the water.

For a moment she was dragged along. Her glove tangled in the nets, and her weakened hand was trapped.

She was pinned against the transom, her arm dragged over the stern, the rest of her body leaning out over *Excelsior*'s wake. Salt spray stung her eyes and her breath caught in her throat. She couldn't scream, and it wouldn't do her any good anyway. Matt wouldn't hear her over the throbbing engines and driving rain.

She had to save herself.

With a desperate wrench, she pulled her hand free of the glove, and hung onto the transom, watching the glove disappear beneath the whitecaps, dragged under by the weight of the net.

The realization that she could have gone over with the net hit her as she dragged herself back into the boat. Her heart hammered in her chest, and her breath came in convulsive gasps.

Matt's hand closed over her shoulder. The unexpected touch nearly stopped her racing heart. She screamed with all the fear that had coursed through her. Clutching Matt's rain-slicked jacket, she shook convulsively. His arms were tight around her, and he held her while she tried to catch her breath and slow the trip-hammer beat of her heart.

"I saw it," he yelled over the wind. "But by the time I could get to you, you were already free."

Sara nodded, her head pressed against Matt's jacket. She still couldn't speak.

"I set the autopilot," Matt said. "I'll finish the nets. Go inside."

Without speaking, Sara made her way to the wheelhouse. *Excelsior* was riding the swells, the steady note of her engines like the beating of a giant heart deep in her hold.

Within minutes, Matt joined her in the wheelhouse. His face was pale, rain dripping down his nose and chin. He glanced at the charts and instruments, then turned to Sara.

"Were you hurt?"

For the first time, Sara looked at her bare hand. There was a scrape around the wrist where the elastic had tried to hold the glove on her hand. Otherwise, her hand was unmarked.

She shook her head. Words stuck in her throat, refusing to leave her mouth.

Matt stepped back to the wheel and adjusted the course. "We'll troll through, and then haul the nets," he said, almost as though talking to himself.

Sara leaned her back against the wall, letting her weight sag for a minute. Yes, she'd had a close call. It had scared them both. But they had work to do. This was no time to fall apart.

She forced herself upright, willing her legs to hold her as the boat rode over another swell.

"I'm sorry," she said. Her voice was quiet, but it didn't quaver. "That was stupid. I should be more careful."

"Mistakes happen to everyone," Matt answered. "We were lucky this time, but let's not push it."

His voice was flat, but Sara knew he had been as frightened as she. They both knew the horror stories, the men that didn't come back.

"Let's not."

"Good plan."

Sara stood quietly for a few minutes, letting her breath return to normal. She was first hot and then cold, as the adrenaline rush passed. Her heart slowed, and at last she was able to take a long, deep breath.

"Well. So that's what it's like."

Matt gave her a sharp look. "What?"

"I've been worried that I'd do something really stupid." She shrugged, the gesture lost in the over-sized rain gear she wore. "Now I've done it and I don't have to worry about when it'll happen. It's sort of like waiting for the first scratch on your new car."

She managed a lop-sided grin, realizing that she really meant it. Now that the awful thing had happened, and she had survived, her confidence was returning, and growing. She could do this. "Do you want me to take the helm or haul the nets?"

Matt seemed to catch her confidence, and returned a small grin. "You better drive. You need two gloves for nets, and you seem to be missing one."

"I have spares," she said.

"Good. You'll need them later."

Matt showed her the course, and helped her set the heading. Together, they figured the throttle setting, then Matt headed for the stern.

Sara's arms ached, but she held the wheel steady. She stood a little straighter and held her chin up. She had done this yesterday, she could do it today. And she could do it tomorrow, and the day after that, for as long as she had to.

Chapter 13

Matt bent his back to the work of hauling the nets back on board and emptying them of their load of rockfish. He was grateful for the ancient SONAR that helped him pinpoint the location of the fish and set the depth for his nets. It might not be foolproof, but it helped.

Once the nets were stowed, Matt sagged against the motionless spool. In his hand was Sara's missing glove, retrieved from the tangle of the net. He stared at it. He had refused to acknowledge the terror that gripped him when he thought Sara was going over, but now he needed a minute to face it. She was safe, she had saved herself. But what about the next time?

By the time he returned to the wheelhouse, his fears were buried where Sara couldn't see them. He would have to be more careful from here on. Another mistake could kill them both.

Sara was at the wheel, her grip more relaxed than it had been the day before. She seemed to have gained her sea legs sometime in the long afternoon. Her face was calm, her back straight and tall.

Sara lifted her face to look at Matt. The familiar undercurrent of strength, of stubbornness and resolve was clear, and she met his gaze. Her mouth was firm, and her lips no longer quivered.

Unable to resist, Matt bent to kiss her. Her lips were soft and inviting. Her lips responded to his, and her mouth came alive.

Matt held her close, the kiss lingering on their lips. For one long minute he was able to ignore the demands of the boat and the fish.

Tiny flickers of excitement ran through Matt's body and converged on his crotch. He ignored them, keeping his mouth gentle and his touch light. For now all he wanted to do was hold Sara in his arms, to know that she was safe.

The radio crackled with static, then a distress call came through, breaking the moment. "Pan-Pan, Pan-Pan, Pan-Pan. This is the vessel *Eugene Five.* We have one person in the water, approximately twenty-five miles north northwest of Astoria. GPS is out, location data unavailable. Requesting assistance. *Eugene Five* standing by. Over."

Matt released Sara and grabbed the radio mike. "*Eugene Five,* this is *Excelsior*. We should be within a few miles, will try to reach you. Over." He revved the engine and headed north.

Finding another small boat on the open ocean was tricky, but he knew the *Eugene Five,* and where she was likely to be. With luck he could help the Coast Guard locate her and rescue the person in the water. For an instant he remembered the terror he had felt. That could have been him on the radio and Sara in the water.

Matt pushed *Excelsior,* running her engines hard and fast. Sara stood at his side, and he could see the concern and uncertainty in her face. "We're obligated to answer the call," he explained. "If we can help without putting ourselves in danger, we have to."

Sara nodded. "I remember now. It's one of the rules. What can I do to help?"

"Just stay here with me and keep a lookout. They should be close. We seem to end up in the same area a lot."

"*Eugene Five,* this is Coast Guard Station *Astoria*. Switch and answer Channel two two alpha, two two alpha. Over."

"Coast Guard this is *Eugene Five*. Switching to two two alpha. Over."

Matt nodded at Sara, and she switched the radio dial to channel twenty-two. The conversation continued between the *Eugene Five* and the Coast Guard station. There was one man in the water, and another crew member was trying to get a life ring to him. As he listened, Matt could imagine the tension on board the *Eugene Five.*

"There!" Sara shouted, pointing at a speck in the distance. "There's something out there."

"*Eugene Five,* this is *Excelsior*. Can you fire a flare? I think we've spotted you. Over."

"Roger that *Excelsior*. Hang tight for just a minute. Over."

The seconds ticked by as they waited, the silence in the tiny wheelhouse stretching like taffy in sunshine. Finally, a puff of orange smoke appeared above the speck, and the radio crackled again.

"Did you get that *Excelsior?*"

"Sure did," Matt replied. "We'll be there in a few minutes."

"Coast Guard *Astoria*," he continued, "We are in visual contact with *Eugene Five*. I repeat, we are in visual contact with *Eugene Five*. They are approximately seven miles north of us, and a couple degrees west."

He read the longitude and latitude from the GPS, and listened as the Coast Guard operator repeated them to the flight crew waiting aboard a helicopter. Help was on the way.

Within minutes, the heavy beating of the rotor blades echoed across the water. The bright orange chopper passed overhead, angling in on the *Eugene Five*. "*Excelsior*, this is Coast Guard *Astoria*. We now have visual contact with Eugene Five. We'll take it from here. Thanks for your help."

"Roger, Coast Guard. *Excelsior* out."

Matt switched the radio frequency, cut the engines back to an idle, and leaned over the wheel. This was a little more excitement than he wanted in his life. And the day wasn't over yet.

Chapter 14

Matt checked his chart again. They had run farther north than he had planned. First to stay ahead of the weather, then to follow the fish, and finally to answer the distress call of the *Eugene Five*. Now they were off the southern Washington coast, near Westport.

Matt considered his options. If they turned for home now, they could run straight back to Newport, and offload the fish in the morning. If they got through the weather. But if they continued north, they might get one more day of fishing, and he knew a couple places in Washington where he could get as good a price as at home.

His Washington permits were current, and that helped him make up his mind. They had a decent catch, but another half day could make a big difference in their pay. He looked at the sun, figuring they might make one more drag before calling it a day.

"We're going up a little farther," he told Sara. "See if we can get one more chance today. Then we'll anchor in a cove I know about." He gave her a wicked little grin. "I think you'll like it."

Matt had discovered Pelican Bay when he was a teenager, helping his dad on a run up the Olympic Peninsula. It was off their usual route, and over the years he had seldom had reason to stop there. But it seemed the ideal place to spend a night with Sara. The sheltered bay was surrounded by the dense rain forest of the Peninsula, and there wasn't a light to be seen for miles. The stars were as beautiful as anywhere he had ever been.

• • •

When Matt spotted another school of rockfish, Sara started her routine again. The rain had stopped, and she had recovered the lost glove.

For the first few minutes she was acutely aware of every movement of the boat and the nets, but she soon relaxed. She fell into a rhythm as she fed the nets over the transom: lift, spread, release, adjust the float, lift, spread, release. Her arms moved automatically, and her legs adjusted to the roll of the deck without conscious thought. She was becoming a fisherman.

She switched places with Matt, taking the helm with renewed confidence. As he handed over the wheel, she saw a faint smile turning up the corners of his mouth.

"What?" she asked.

"You."

"What do you mean, 'You'?"

"Just, you."

"Matt! Make sense."

He shrugged and headed out of the wheelhouse. He stopped in the doorway, and turned back to look at her. "You're turning into a fisherman." He grinned and went out.

Sara wanted to throw her hands in the air and follow him, to tell him that this wasn't some kind of joke. Instead she kept her hands on the wheel, and her concentration on the course heading.

After a moment, she smiled. He had said exactly what she had thought a few minutes before. A flush of pride washed through her, and she stood a little taller. Matt thought she was turning into a fisherman. Maybe, if she didn't make any more stupid mistakes, they had found a solution, temporarily, for their money troubles. Maybe she was becoming a real partner, not just the wife who waited at home.

After Matt hauled the nets in, he came forward to the wheelhouse and relieved her. "Almost a full load. Black rockfish, with damn little bycatch."

Sara shot him a puzzled look.

"Other kinds of fish. *Fish and Wildlife* keeps track of that stuff. This catch looks pretty clean." He smiled, and Sara breathed a sigh of relief. Their first trip was almost over, and it looked like a success.

"It'll take a little while to reach Pelican Bay," he said. "Why don't you grab a shower, and maybe get a nap? You look beat."

"I thought I was doing pretty well." But even she could hear the exhaustion in her voice, and she was imagining the luxury of hot water and soap.

"You're doing great. I couldn't ask for a better view, er, crew. Really."

"Which is it?"

"Either one. Both." His voice dropped the teasing note, turning solemn. "You did a good job out here today. You worked hard, and you kept your head when things went bad. I'm really proud of you."

Sara felt a blush creep up her cheeks. Matt wasn't given to lavish praise, and his words meant a lot. She lowered her eyes to hide the fact that they were brimming with tears. She blinked them away, and looked up at Matt.

"Thanks, honey." She raised on tiptoe and planted a little kiss on his cheek. "Are you serious about the shower?"

"Absolutely. You remember how to set the controls?"

"Some things are far too important to forget," she teased back.

He reached down and patted her bottom.

"Then get some rest while you can. This trip isn"t over yet." The teasing tone had returned, and the solemn moment had passed.

Sara surrendered to the temptations of hot water and sleep. She lowered herself down the ladder, her eyes beginning to droop in anticipation of a nap.

● ● ●

"You stay right there. It's my turn to fix dinner." Matt's voice came through a drowsy fog, and Sara pried her eyes open. The cabin was dark, with only a couple battery lights on. The curtains were drawn tight against the dark. Inside and out, the night was silent. The engines were shut down, and even the generator was turned off.

Sara raised herself on one elbow, stopping short of hitting her head on the low ceiling of the bunk. Matt threw her a kiss and disappeared into the head. Sara heard the shower start and stop, and she could imagine Matt, his body slick and shiny. She drifted into a fantasy of a wet, naked Matt, smiling at the images her mind created.

When Matt returned a few minutes later, dry and fully dressed, he began to assemble their meal. In the cooler he dug out eggs and cheese, and bread from the cupboard. Within minutes, the smell of cheese omelets filled the dim cabin, tickling Sara's nose into wakefulness.

"When you're ready, you can climb down from there. These should be done in a couple minutes." Matt waved the frying pan, then returned it to the flame.

Dragging the threadbare blanket that she had wrapped around herself, Sara crawled down onto the hard bench. She tugged at the legs of her sweats where they had twisted around her in her sleep. She yawned, and curled back into the corner of the bench.

Matt put their plates on the table, and sat down next to her. He gave her a quick squeeze, and a quick kiss. "Hungry?"

She nodded, and gave him a tired grin. "Somehow," she said, "I seem to have worked up an appetite."

Matt nodded in agreement and they dug into the omelets. Matt seldom cooked at home, and Sara was impressed with the food.

"Where'd you learn to cook?"

"Somebody has to out here, or else you end up living on peanut butter sandwiches made with stale bread. Josh's idea of gourmet cooking was to add dried onion to a can of cheap chili." Matt wrinkled his nose at the memory of Josh's so-called meals.

"So how come I never heard about this talent?"

"Are you kidding? Then you'd expect me to cook at home."

Sara cocked an eyebrow at him. "You say that like it's a bad thing."

"Believe me," Matt answered around a mouthful of omelet, "it is. Omelets are one of about three things that I can cook. I think you'd get tired of them real quick. I know I do."

"Then maybe I ought to teach you a few new ones."

"Or we could take turns with the cooking."

"There is that," Sara said. "But I like the idea of a husband who cooks."

• • •

They were silent then, hunger and exhaustion crowding out conversation as they ate. Matt was getting used to having Sara on board, and he found he liked the arrangement. The way she was today, he'd almost rather have her on board than Josh. Besides she looked better, and smelled better, than Josh ever did.

Sara sighed and pushed her plate away. Her eyes were drooping, and Matt suspected she would be ready to sleep again soon. He finished the last of his food, stacking his plate on top of hers. He would take care of the dishes in a few minutes. But right now he felt too content to move.

Putting his arm around Sara, Matt pulled her back against his chest and rested her head under his chin. He marveled at how well she fit in his arms. She always had, and he hoped she always would.

Matt dozed, Sara cradled in his embrace. She was warm and soft, and he squeezed her to him. She snuggled her back against his chest, and he heard a little contented sigh.

"Comfy?" he asked.

"Mmm-hmmm." She settled against him, her arms across her chest, resting on top of his. Matt knew they would have to move, if only to crawl up into the bunk. Later.

Chapter 15

Matt put a finger under Sara's chin and tilted her head back. She smiled up at him, and he bent down to kiss her lips. She felt warm and sleepy, and her mouth yielded to his. Their mouths lingered, lips soft and undemanding.

Sara could feel Matt's heart beating. He pulled her tighter, the kiss deepened and she parted her lips, inviting him to explore her mouth.

The boat rocked gently in the calm of the sheltered cove, and she clung to Matt. Her body stirred in response to his kiss. She leaned against him, her hands holding his. Her mouth no longer yielded and accepted, it demanded. She caught his bottom lip between her teeth, tugging and sucking.

She released his mouth, and turned back to look at Matt. His eyes were tender, but she could see the beginning of desire. He bent to her mouth and possessed it, the passion spreading from him to her, sending excitement racing through her body.

The swiftness of her reaction surprised Sara. One minute she had been dozing against Matt's chest. The next, she was kissing him passionately, their tongues dancing, darting, tasting. She was flooded with desire, and her entire body ached for his touch.

Sara turned to reach Matt's shirt, and began to undo the buttons. His tongue explored her mouth, his teeth tugged at her lips.

For a moment the flush of passion receded, and she struggled with the buttons, finally succeeding in baring his chest. She could smell the saltwater on his skin — the residue of their long day, and the familiar mix of odors that was Matt. It nearly overwhelmed her, making her head spin with the power of her desire. She moaned, a faint hum against the onslaught of Matt's tongue and teeth.

His arms still held her, crushed against his body, her hands on his chest trapped between their bodies. She wanted, needed, him to touch her, to feed her consuming hunger. She wanted him to possess all of her, to claim her body and satisfy her need.

She moved in his embrace, trying to expose her body to his touch. He seemed to understand the desperate signal her body sent, and his hands began to roam across her. He ran his hands along her back, palms flat, as though to maximize the contact. He released one arm from her, and stroked her side, from neck to knee. It was torture, sheer and exquisite. He touched none of the parts that ached for his caress, yet every nerve in her body tingled in response, and her pulse throbbed.

Sara's heart was racing now, her skin burned, and she couldn't get enough air to fill her lungs. Her head was too heavy for her neck to support, lolling against Matt's chest, where she could feel the pounding of his heart, answering her own.

Her hands moved without any conscious plan on her part, sweeping across the broad planes of his chest and around his back. She buried her face in his neck, nipping at the tender skin. Matt's hand stopped in its travels along her side, gripping her thigh as the swift rush of desire swept over him.

As his grip loosened slightly, and his hand started to move again, she nipped once more. His hands instantly tightened into fists and his body stiffened, pushing against her.

Sara tried to turn, to reach more of Matt's body. But the confines of the tiny bench were too much. There was no place to turn, no room to maneuver. Frustration rose within her, forcing its way out in a whimper.

"What, what is it?" Matt's voice was raspy, his breath ragged.

"No room." Sara wiggled against him. She sighed, and tried again, but there really was no room. She was trapped in the corner, the table an effective barrier to any movement.

Matt saw the problem and lunged from behind the table. With an impatient toss, he sent the abandoned dishes into the miniature sink. The table disappeared against the wall, and Sara was free to move.

Matt was standing in front of Sara, the front of his jeans bulging with the hard evidence of his desire. Without thought, without planning, she reached for him. She opened his jeans with desperate fingers, releasing his erection into her waiting hands and mouth.

The jolt of contact shook Matt, and he grabbed the side of the bunk above her head to keep from falling. She could feel him shaking, his knees weak. He throbbed in her mouth, the soft skin rubbing against her tongue.

She stopped, holding him trembling on the edge, then she began to stroke him, taking the length of his shaft into her mouth, letting her tongue slide along the underside, until he filled her. With deliberate slowness, she released him, her lips sliding back down until she held just the sensitive tip in her mouth.

With one hand, she reached between his legs and squeezed his scrotum. Matt's legs stiffened, and he pressed himself against her mouth. She opened to him, taking him deep in her throat once again, then releasing him with the same tantalizing slowness.

Sara knew what Matt liked. Her daring in giving it unasked, and his reaction, fed her growing excitement. The satisfaction of giving him intense pleasure surged through her as she lowered her mouth around him once again. He bucked against her, letting go of the bunk to wind his hands in her hair. She could feel him growing, longer and harder with every stroke.

Matt gave a groan and released her hair. He pulled himself from her mouth, and dropped to his knees in front of her.

"This isn't fair," he moaned, taking her in his arms. "It's one-sided and selfish."

"No," Sara answered, reveling in the feeling of power. "Not if I enjoy it." She kissed him, and her hand reached between them, once again closing around his shaft.

He reached for her hand and put it at her side. "My turn," he said through gritted teeth. He pulled the sweatshirt over her head, and yanked her pants over her hips. She wore nothing underneath, and within moments she sat naked on the bench in front of him.

Matt knelt between her legs, and pulled her into his embrace. She wrapped her legs around him, and her lips found his. Their kiss was intense, and Matt's hands found her breasts. The sensation was instant and overwhelming. Sara cried out as he touched the hard, sensitive nipples, holding them tightly in his fingers. She arched her back, pushing their engorged points against his hands.

Matt lowered his face from her mouth to her nipples. He licked and sucked and held them in his teeth, teasing and tormenting. His hands gripped her breasts, squeezing with the rhythm of his sucking.

Sara wrapped her legs tighter around Matt and pressed her crotch against his chest. She rubbed her swollen lips against the hard slab of muscle and whimpered with the desire to get closer. She was wet with excitement.

Matt pushed her back on the bench, propping her feet on the edge and leaving her exposed. His tongue trailed down her chest, darting around her navel. He held her thighs open, one hand on each knee, and looked at her glistening lips. "Beautiful," he said, and buried his face in her crotch.

She felt the exquisite sensation of his tongue licking her slit. He sucked at her lips, and teased the mouth of her vagina with tiny thrusts of his tongue.

She slid her hips forward, spreading her legs wide and opening herself to his busy mouth. Matt slid one hand from her knee to her crotch, plunging his fingers inside her and causing her to cry out.

His hand was wet with her juices, and she could see him reaching between his legs to rub them on his erection. He moaned at the touch, a humming vibration against her swollen lips that drove her higher.

His darting tongue traveled from her vagina to her clitoris, rubbing over the hard nub. Sara stiffened, pushing her hips forward, rocking against Matt's probing tongue.

Matt found her rhythm, and began his relentless attention to the tiny erection. His tongue probed and licked. Sara's hands crept across her chest, and squeezed her breasts. As Matt's tongue rubbed her clitoris, her fingers echoed the movement on her nipples.

She was close, her body shaking with need. Matt moved his hand back to her crotch, and plunged his fingers deep into her trembling vagina. She raised her lips to meet his thrust, squeezing him tight, pressing herself hard against his mouth. A cry tore from her throat, and her hips pumped as her climax tore through her.

She was shaking with release. Matt continued, his lips and tongue now soft and gentle, for another minute. Then, instead of letting go and crawling up onto the bench with her, Matt sat back a little and took both her hands in his. He tugged her off the bench and lay back, pulling her down over him.

Sara hesitated for a moment. This was new, and she was uncertain. She had never been very adventurous, but Matt's hands cupped her ass and pressed her against his stiff penis.

He put his hands on her thighs, pulling them around him, and guiding her until she settled over him. He bucked and sighed, a sound of such contentment that Sara wondered for a moment if he had already climaxed. But another quick upward thrust of his body assured her that was not the case.

He held her hips, pulling her against him. She could feel him pushing into her, filling her in a new way. It was exciting and different, and his hands urged her to move against him.

Unsure of herself in this new position, she felt awkward. As an experiment, she lifted her body slightly, drawing away, then lowered herself again. The force of his answering thrust reassured and pleasured her at the same time. She repeated the movement and was rewarded with another surge of pleasure. Matt groaned out her name, urging her on.

His hand rode her hips for a minute, helping her establish a rhythm that drove him higher. Then he released her hips and reached for her breasts. His fingers closed around them, and he squeezed.

Pleasure surged through Sara, and she rocked against him. Grinding her hips against Matt, she felt her excitement grow. She was close to coming again.

Before she could reach her climax, she felt Matt stiffen beneath her, and she heard him moan. His body bucked, his hips driving up into her. She clung to him, her hands gripping his shoulders, squeezing and holding, urging him on. She matched his rhythm as best she could, following the urging of his hands that once again gripped her hips.

Matt bucked once more and groaned. She watched his face as his climax took him over the top, saw the completion sweep over him. His grip loosened, and she felt his erection begin to subside.

She rocked against his crotch for a few seconds longer, unwilling to stop. In the faint light, she saw the sudden concern on Matt's face. Rocking, she drew a deep breath and concentrated, willing herself to completion.

She couldn't do it, but she hid it from Matt with a shiver and a long sigh, and collapsed against his chest. Her lips were still swollen, pressing against her hard clitoris. She knew the feeling would subside. Matt had given her great pleasure, and this would be better next time. But for now she was uncomfortably aware of her unfulfilled desires.

For long minutes the cabin was still and quiet. The only sound was their labored breathing, the only movement the slowing gallop of their hearts. Sara lay soft and warm against Matt, forcing herself to ignore the ache in her groin.

Matt lay beneath her, relaxed and content. Although he could have moved, he didn't act like he wanted to. They drifted along on their contentment, slow murmurs and sighs passing between them, without words.

Chapter 16

Little by little, Matt began to come back to life. The rough rubber mat on the floor was digging into his back. His bare skin was being rubbed by the tiny nubs designed to clean boots. He would pay for this little adventure, but it had been worth the price.

Holding Sara with one arm, Matt reached up and dragged the blanket down, wrapping it over her naked back. He rolled her over with a gentle nudge, her tender skin now protected by the soft cushion of blanket. He tucked the end around her, forming a warm cocoon with his wife inside. That done, he stood up.

His knees were wobbly, and it took him a moment to recover his sea legs. Once his balance had returned, he bent to pick up Sara, and gently sat her on the bench. He sat beside her and wrapped his arms around her. She gave a soft sigh and snuggled into the cocoon Matt had made for her.

"Relax, darling." He stroked her face, and watched a drowsy smile light her eyes. Matt felt a surge of pride, some primitive instinct telling him he was a man, and this was his woman. He had claimed her, taken her, and she was his prize. His civilized brain reminded him this was probably not a thought he should share with the independent, stubborn woman he had married.

That was one of the things he found fascinating about his wife — the stubbornness and resolve that supported her throughout her life. If she decided to do something, nothing could get in her way.

In the last couple days, Sara had been more sexually daring than he had ever seen her. Their lovemaking tonight, trying a new position, was proof of that. She might not be the outright aggressor, but she was certainly loosening up.

Life aboard ship was beginning to look very interesting. He let his eyelids droop, savoring the warmth and softness of Sara's body. Just a few minutes more...

The sound of a diesel engine cut through the stillness. It was faint but unmistakable, and Matt was instantly alert. He fought back the surge of adrenaline, telling himself that it was just a stray fisherman, passing up the coast. It might be late, but maybe the guy was anxious to get home.

Instead of receding as the boat passed the mouth of Pelican Bay, however, the noise grew louder. The boat was coming into the bay. Their private evening was over.

He nudged Sara's shoulder, and whispered in her ear. "There's another boat coming in the bay. We need to get dressed, before they see us."

Sara shot up. Startled from her doze, her eyes widened with surprise. "It there trouble?" she whispered, her voice sleepy and faint.

"No, no. Nothing like that. I just figured you wouldn't want to meet another crew without your pants on."

"Oh!" Sara clutched the blanket to her chest, as though just remembering she was naked. She fumbled around her, trying to find her missing clothes in the dim glow of a single battery light. Matt swallowed the chuckle that rose in his throat, as he tried to find his own pants. He saw Sara make a face at the wadded-up mass of her sweats, and grab her jeans and a shirt.

The noise of the diesel was much louder now, echoing across the broad bay and bouncing off the surrounding trees.

Matt didn't know why, or what it was, but something didn't seem right. He just knew that after all the years he had spent at sea, this boat, in this bay, on this night, didn't feel right. The deep throb of the engines didn't sound like a coastal fisherman, and Pelican Bay was off the normal fishing routes.

He was here because he had gone out of his way to spend a romantic evening with his wife. But no one else should even be out here. He slapped at the battery light, plunging the cabin into total darkness.

Normally Matt would have grabbed a pair of jeans and gone topside to hail the other skipper. But this time he hesitated. He took a long time buttoning his jeans and digging around for a shirt. He found socks, and dragged them over his feet, then went searching for his deck shoes. He felt a great reluctance to venture out. He was relieved that the engines were shut down and they had not shown any light, grateful that the intruders hadn't noticed them.

Sara bumped into Matt in the dark and gave him a quick kiss. "Are you going out there?"

Her voice sounded loud in the tiny cabin, and he shushed her without thinking.

"It is trouble," she whispered. "Why else would you be so jumpy?"

Matt shrugged. He knew she couldn't really see the gesture in the dark, but it was a natural reaction. "I dunno. There's just something about another boat in this bay."

He tried to sort out why it felt wrong, and couldn't find a reason he could put into words. He shook his head. If he kept this up, he'd be telling her it was intuition. "It's probably nothing, just jumpy because I dozed off." He yawned and stretched. "Give me a few minutes to wake up, then we'll go up and hail them, see who it is."

Sara nodded, and Matt could barely discern the movement of her head. His eyes had adjusted a little more, and he could move about the cabin more easily.

He took Sara by the hand, and led her back to the bench. "I'm going to sit down and let my brain wake up, okay?"

Two minutes passed, then three and four. He could hear the engines of the intruder cut back, the voices of the crew calling to one another. There were a lot of voices, far more than would be expected for another fishing vessel. Maybe it was a power sailer, off course and trying to find a sheltered spot to spend the night.

Curious, Matt crept to the small window and pulled the curtain aside. On the far side of the bay, a dark-painted trawler, about twice their size, rocked in the tiny swells. A pair of crewmen stood on deck, their faces lit by the glow of their cigarettes. Another crewman stood by the winch, paying out the anchor chain. Running lights and deck lights drew the ship in sharp contrast to the blackness of the night that surrounded her.

Matt worked the lever on the window, and swung it open a crack. He could hear the deep voices of the men on deck, the harsh sound of words he couldn't make out. The sound carried across the water, now that the trawler's engines were slowed, but he had to strain to hear their conversation. The crew on the other side of the bay was speaking a foreign language. It sounded like Russian. He could not understand a single word, and the thought made him uneasy.

He pulled the window closed and silently thanked God that he had shut everything down. There could be an innocent explanation, but he didn't want to take chances, not with Sara aboard.

He stepped back from the window, blinded by the lights on the trawler. He held his hands in front of himself and made his way back to the bench.

"I don't think we should go out right now," he whispered. "It looks like a foreign trawler. The guys on deck aren't speaking English. I'll bet it's just some poor schmuck who was inside territorial waters and wanted a place to hide for the night. But if it is, they aren't going to want company."

He felt Sara stiffen, and her hand clamped around his arm. "Then what do we do?"

"We don't do anything," he replied, patting her hand where it gripped his arm.

"Shouldn't we call the Coast Guard?"

"What for? They haven't done anything."

"But you said they didn't speak English — "

"Last I checked, that wasn't a crime. And even if they aren't supposed to be here, what's the harm? We just wait. When they haul anchor in the morning, they'll assume we're asleep, and be grateful to get the hell away. We let 'em. Sort of like meeting a bear in the woods — let 'em retreat, and don't mess with them."

They sat in silence, the sound of the other boat muffled by the closed windows and doors, but still discernible. It seemed like an eternity before quiet began to drift back over the bay. The diesels were throttled back to a low idle, and the voices had stopped calling.

Matt was about to suggest they turn in and wait for morning, when he heard the throb of another, smaller, diesel. He hurried to the window to see what was causing the noise.

Matt surveyed the scene across the bay. A fishing boat had joined the trawler. A huge bear of a man emerged from the trawler's wheelhouse, and gestured to someone on the fishing boat. Matt's heart sank and his blood ran cold as he recognized the *Janice Lee.*

Sara's hand on his shoulder startled him. He bit his lip to keep from yelling at her, but his stomach knotted with the strain of containing his impulse.

"What's going on? I heard another boat."

"They're meeting someone out there. But we're fine, they don't know we're here. If they did, they would have come after us before now."

Sara's sharp intake of breath told him that, despite his attempts to soften the impact, she was getting scared.

"Besides," he continued, trying to calm her, "with their lights on like that, they can't see anything past the spot that's illuminated. It's so dark around them, they'll never know we're here."

Matt crossed his fingers and hoped he was right. He knew this stuff, they really couldn't see anything beyond their lights. But what would happen if they switched them off? And what would happen when the sun came up and they found that they were not alone? He tried not to think about that.

Sara turned back to the window, trying to peer over Matt's broad shoulder. "So what is going on out there?"

When Matt hesitated, Sara gripped his upper arm and shook him. "Dammit, Matt. Let me see. It's better to know what's going on than it is to sit and imagine the worst. Or haven't you figured that out by now?"

Matt moved to the side, allowing her to share the narrow view across the water.

The *Janice Lee* pulled alongside the trawler, and a tall man with dark hair scrambled agilely up the ladder that was thrown over the side. Matt recognized Marty Green, skipper of the *Janice Lee.* Marty shook hands with the bear-man, whom Matt assumed was the captain of the trawler. The captain pushed a small suitcase toward Marty, who opened it on the deck and examined the contents. His back was to Matt, shielding the open suitcase from view.

Matt glanced at the fishing boat pulled alongside the trawler. He spotted Harry Yost, a school pal who had recently signed on as first mate of the *Janice Lee,* watching from the railing below. Curious, Matt opened the window. As he watched, Marty nodded and closed the suitcase. He shook the captain's hand, and jumped back onto the deck of the *Janice Lee.* Gesturing at his watch, Marty yelled "Two hours." He waved to Harry to get underway, the diesels spooled up, and the boat headed for the mouth of the bay.

"What is it?" Sara whispered, her voice worried. Matt couldn't blame her for that, he was plenty worried, too. They didn't belong in the middle of this, whatever it was, and there was no place to go, no way to retreat from the much larger boat in the pool of light across the bay.

Without answering, Matt latched the window and let the curtain drop.

"Shouldn't we call somebody?" Sara continued. "This is a state park, isn't it? We could call the park rangers. Or the Coast Guard, or the Navy? Somebody?" Her voice was high and tight, her fear building. He had to do something, quick.

Not knowing what else he could do, Matt grabbed Sara and kissed her. She stiffened, then returned the kiss, as though forgetting for a moment the drama unfolding across the bay. He could feel her tension level drop, and her fear subsided. When he released her a moment later, she had to lean against him to keep her balance.

"What was that for?" she whispered.

"To take your mind off the trawler, and calm you down. You were getting pretty wound up." He smiled in the dark. "Worked, too, didn't it?"

Sara, hearing the grin in his voice, gave him a light punch him in the arm. "Maybe, but you don't have to be so smug about it." She laid her hand on Matt's arm, rubbing the spot she had just punched. "Okay, I'm calmer. But I am serious. Shouldn't we call somebody?"

"Sara," Matt whispered, "the only way to call anyone is to use the radio. And I'll just bet you those guys are scanning every radio frequency on the dial, especially the emergency ones." He covered her hand with his, squeezing it for reassurance.

"Marty said 'two hours.' That means he'll be back. We could make a run for it while they're waiting, but I'm betting they would follow us. They're bigger and more powerful, and they won't have a few tons of ice and fish slowing them down."

He felt her fingers clench around his, but she nodded her head. He pulled her by the hand back to the bench, and sat with his arm around her shoulders.

"Matt?" Sara's voice was soft, but steady.

"Yes, honey?"

"We can't just sit here like this for two hours or more. You ought to take a nap." She put her fingers over his lips, stifling his protest. Her voice was firm. "I mean it. If we're going to wait, at least get some good from it. I got a nap this afternoon. You need some rest. I can watch these guys. And I promise, cross my heart, to call you if they do anything."

Reluctant, though he knew she was right, he agreed. He didn't want Sara to take the responsibility for watching the trawler, but he was tired.

Before crawling into the bunk, he found a bucket for Sara to sit on, and put the cushion from the bench on top of it. It wasn't much, but she could sit next to the window and keep an eye on the antics of the crew across the bay.

Matt wasn't sure he would be able to stop worrying enough to sleep. But as soon as he lay down, his eyelids began to droop, and his body felt too heavy to move.

Chapter 17

Sara listened as Matt's breathing deepened and slowed. She knew the instant he was asleep. She poured the last of the coffee from the pot and resisted the urge to reheat it. Cold coffee wasn't very appetizing, but the caffeine would help keep her alert.

Balancing on the overturned bucket, Sara held the coffee mug in her clenched hands, and moved the curtain aside, creating a tiny slit through which she could watch the Russians. One of the men — too slender to be the captain — stood at the rail facing *Excelsior*. Sara had the unsettling feeling that the man was looking directly at her, that he could see her eyes in the dark that separated the boats.

Then, in the time-honored tradition of men without women, the man unzipped his trousers and let fly over the side of the boat. His crewmates found this hilarious in the extreme. Soon the other two men joined him at the rail. One man carried a bottle that he hefted to his mouth and took a long pull.

The man with the bottle carried it back a couple feet, setting it with exaggerated care on the deck. He returned to the rail, and the good-natured argument continued. They waved their arms with abandon, and though Sara couldn't hear them, the meaning was clear. It was a pissing contest.

The three men retreated from the rail to retrieve the bottle. They passed it back and forth, each one tilting the bottle high. After a couple rounds, one of the men tilted the bottle and found it empty. With an impatient gesture, he tossed the empty into the bay, and retrieved another from the wheelhouse.

She watched the men as they jockeyed around each other, and tried to figure out what their relationship was to one another. The binoculars were in the wheelhouse, and she was timid about going up the ladder. It felt so exposed somehow, to leave the shelter of the cabin.

She remembered seeing a small spyglass, not much more than a child's toy, stuck in the cupboard with the groceries. She had wondered at the time why it was there, but had forgotten to ask Matt about it.

Now, she got up from her perch on the bucket and felt her way to the cupboard. There it was, just behind a large can. She pulled the spyglass from its hiding place.

She held the cupboard latch open and closed the door, slowly releasing the latch, trying to be quiet. The latch clicked as it fell into place, the noise sounding like an explosion in the silence of the cabin. Sara jumped, but she hung onto the glass.

Matt continued his soft snoring, undisturbed by her movements. She crept back to her improvised stool and pulled the curtain back to reveal a narrow view.

She quickly discovered she had to stand back from the window to allow room for the glass. She rearranged her bucket and cushion, and rested the end of the glass against the closed window. She put her eye to the hole and adjusted the focus as best she could.

She could see the men, though the glass lacked the sharp focus of good optics. There were three on deck, and she could see the shadowy figure of a fourth man in the wheelhouse. None of the three on deck were the bear-like man she had seen earlier, the one Matt thought was the captain. He must be the one in the wheelhouse.

It was like watching a foreign movie with a bad soundtrack and no subtitles. She kept the window shut. One reason was to keep the noise from Matt, but another was that this particular soundtrack told her nothing.

As she watched, two of the men appeared to be arguing. The third, a short man with close-cropped dark hair and a broad Slavic face, backed away from the other two, his hands up, palms out. He seemed to be saying that, whatever their argument was, he wanted no part of it.

The two men continued to argue. They looked to be well matched — both tall and deeply muscled, with heavy eyebrows and curly dark hair. One wore his hair long and tied back in an unruly ponytail, the other's was shorter, just reaching the collar of his dirty denim jacket, and shot through with gray.

The longhaired man was younger, she guessed, maybe by eight or ten years, and he seemed to be the aggressor. Something in their posture suggested they knew each other well, and that this argument was a familiar one.

The younger man took a step toward his opponent, waving his arms in wide arcs. The older man stood his ground. His back was to Sara and she couldn't see his face, but the effect was clear. The younger man continued to yell and wave his arms, but he didn't move any closer. With a last, dismissive wave of his hand, he turned his back and walked a few steps away.

That seemed to be what the older one had been waiting for. In two long strides he was close enough to grab him by the back of his jacket, and wrap one long arm around his throat. There was a knife in his other hand, though Sara hadn't seen him pull it.

It was the kind of thing Sara had heard about all her life. Life at sea was harsh, and it attracted a certain percentage of hard-living, hard-drinking men — the kind who would pull a knife or throw a punch without thought, when fueled with enough anger or alcohol.

Everything moved in slow motion while Sara held her breath. The two men stood motionless, as though testing their resolve. She could hear the harsh sound of their voices through the closed window. Would the old man use the knife? Would the young one relent, apologize, maybe beg for his life? She watched, waiting for the next move.

The broad back of the captain appeared in the narrow vision of the glass. The gun in his outstretched hand rested against the older man's graying head, and the world stopped. An immense silence fell over the bay, broken by the faint thumping of the trawler's generator.

Sara gulped air convulsively, her lungs forcing her to breathe. She shuddered and tensed again, staring through the glass. Aboard the trawler, no one had moved, except the man with the bottle, who took a deep drink. She could feel the tension in the scene across the bay, see it in the tight ropes of muscle that stood out in the captain's arm.

The gun stayed planted against the man's temple. The captain's hand was steady, his arm rigid. There was no hesitation, no waver, in his posture.

The captain broke the silence with a barked command. For long seconds, no one responded. Sara's eyes burned with the need to blink. She had an insane impulse to scream and shout, to break the thread of tension that was winding around and around her. She clamped her lips between her teeth, and held on.

The captain spoke again. Even with the window closed, she could hear the commanding tone.

The older man relaxed the arm around the other man's throat. The younger man lunged away from his attacker, rubbing his hand over his throat, as though to erase the crushing pressure he had felt. He turned around, and even at this distance Sara could see fear and anger on his face.

The captain retreated a step, the gun still held steady at the man with the knife. Sara could see his lips moving, but he was talking quietly now, and his voice didn't carry through the closed window. As the captain talked, she saw the fight go out of the man. His shoulders slumped, his arms hung at his sides, and the knife clattered to the deck. His head dipped to his chest, and he was transformed into an old, pathetic drunk, instead of the raving madman of a few minutes earlier.

Her heart raced and her breath was shallow. This was the most frightening thing she had ever experienced. These were angry, violent men who seemed to have no hesitation about using whatever weapons were at hand, and they were between her and Matt, and the open sea. If they were spotted, she was sure they wouldn't leave Pelican Bay alive. She swallowed hard. All she could do was wait and see what happened across the bay. Their lives depended on her staying silent and keeping watch.

Sara bent her head and pushed the button to light the face of her watch. She watched the seconds tick past and the date change as it passed midnight. Marty's two hours were more than half gone. She wondered if she should wake Matt before the *Janice Lee* came back, but decided against it. There wasn't anything he could do that she wasn't already doing, and he operated with an internal alarm that would wake him soon enough.

She continued to stare out the window, keeping her breath light and wiggling her shoulders every few minutes. She was getting cramped, sitting on the bucket. She had developed a pattern, standing for five or ten minutes, until her back ached from bending over, then sitting until her neck hurt from craning up. Her eyes burned all the time, and her face ached from squinting.

She watched the captain prowl the deck, pacing along the perimeter of the boat. He walked with slow, deliberate paces, and appeared to be checking the mooring lines and hatches as he went.

He disappeared behind the wheelhouse, and Sara took her eye away from the glass for a moment. She closed her eyes, which were painfully dry from her surveillance, and sat with her head bowed. She only allowed herself a few seconds of rest, and then returned to watching the trawler.

The captain appeared again at the bow of the trawler, and continued along the near side of the boat. She watched as he tugged on lines, nodding his satisfaction when they held fast. She saw a flash of disgust cross his face as he neared the spot where the men had been fighting. He crouched down and Sara realized he was dogging a hatch on one of the holds. Either it hadn't been made fast, or one of the crew had knocked it loose in their scuffle.

He took a last look around the deck and nodded, as though satisfied. Then he went into the wheelhouse. He lit a lamp, and Sara could see him moving around the wheelhouse. He was little more than a shadow in the dimly lit space, but she shivered as she thought about how exposed she would be, if *Excelsior*'s cabin lights had been lit.

Chapter 18

Sitting alone in the dark, surrounded by the silence of the bay, Sara's thoughts drifted. Matt was asleep in the bunk a few feet away, and the trawler was quiet. All around her, nothing moved, nothing made a sound.

The seat on top of the bucket was hard, pressing against her. She wiggled, trying to rearrange the thin cushion. Instead, she succeeded in bunching it up, creating a ridge that pressed against her crotch. It reminded her of the way Matt's body had pushed against her earlier.

She sighed a little, and shifted her body. The pressure was pleasant, and a little thrill of excitement passed through her. She put one hand to her neck, sliding her fingers over her throat, and down the open collar of her shirt. She caressed her neck and chest with light touches, as she pressed her thighs together, squeezing her crotch.

She stared across the water, the spyglass now abandoned on the floor at her feet. She laid her other arm across her body, cradling her breasts. She wasn't touching them, just resting them against her arm.

She thought about what Matt had done earlier. It had felt good, the way his erection had pressed up into her, and the way her body had opened and covered him. She rocked on the cushion, remembering his hard thrusts.

She continued to stare out the window, as if denying the touch of her busy fingers, now creeping across her breasts and rubbing her nipples. Excitement built at her touch, and she squeezed her breast, stifling a moan.

She stopped, and listened for a moment to Matt snoring, then her fingers continued their exploration. She slipped a hand between the buttons of her shirt, savoring the feel of her soft breast against her fingers. A squeeze, a pinch, and her crotch tingled with excitement.

Her other hand rested against her leg, and her fingers rubbed little circles on the worn denim on the inside of her thigh. She spread her legs and leaned forward, pressing her crotch against the cushion, the way she had pressed against Matt. As she imagined his hard shaft inside her, her lips swelled and her clitoris began to throb.

Her breath was ragged, and she held her bottom lip between her teeth, forcing herself to remain silent. She teased herself, undoing the buttons of her shirt and brushing one hand lightly over her breasts, while the other rubbed and kneaded her thighs through her jeans.

She squeezed her breast, then released it, and unbuttoned her jeans, letting the zipper slide down. She slid her hand inside, rubbing her soft belly, and brushing her fingertips over the coarse hair that covered her mound.

Sara leaned back, tilting her hips, allowing her fingers to slip lower. Her other hand clutched at her thigh, then crept up to fondle her breasts.

She stretched one finger out and slipped it into her crack, now slick with her juices. She could feel her throbbing erection, a miniature of Matt's. She rubbed her finger over it, sliding her hand over her mound, and plunging her fingers into her aching vagina.

She could feel the muscles clamp around her fingers, feeding her arousal through her hand and her crotch. Her fingers wiggled, sending intense pleasure through her. She pressed her fingers deeper, pumping them in and out, and rested her thumb on her swollen clitoris.

As she continued to slide her fingers in and out, her thumb made tiny circles around the hard nub, pushing the wet folds of her lips back and forth across its sensitive surface. With each circle, Sara felt her arousal grow, until she knew her climax was inevitable.

She slowed her fingers, relaxing the pressure, savoring the feeling of intense desire. But she couldn't hold back, couldn't wait long. With a desperate hunger, she plunged her fingers deep inside her. Her thumb rubbed harder and faster, and her other hand squeezed her breast. Her muscles contracted, her legs stiffened, and one last, intense burst of sensation sent her soaring into a shuddering climax.

She bit her lips to muffle her moans. Her fingers continued to stroke her lips, gentle rubbing and patting, as her arousal subsided. Her muscles relaxed, and she sagged against the bulkhead.

Matt stirred in the bunk, startling her. She zipped her jeans and buttoned her shirt with fingers that still trembled with her release. But Matt began to snore again, and Sara relaxed. She sighed as the tension drained from her body. She loved her husband, and she enjoyed their lovemaking, but sometimes she couldn't quite explain what she wanted. This time, she had been daring enough to do something about it. Somehow, the self-confidence she was gaining on deck had followed her below.

The respite didn't last long. Within minutes, she could hear the sound of diesels in the distance. It would be *Janice Lee* returning. Matt was right, they didn't know anything, but she was convinced this meeting in a secluded cove in the middle of the night didn't have an innocent explanation.

Although she was back to concentrating on the trawler, she heard the change in Matt's breathing. He was no longer deeply asleep, snoring softly in the bunk. His breathing was less regular, and he was tossing in his sleep. In a few minutes, she knew, he would be awake.

She put the end of the glass back against the window, and squinted. The men were moving around on the deck of the trawler, although the two fighters were avoiding each other. The sound of the diesels grew louder, and soon she could see the running lights as they entered the bay.

The smaller boat pulled alongside the trawler, maneuvering close and throwing two lines up. The older man caught the bowline and made it fast to a cleat on deck, while the younger one tied off the stern. A ladder was dropped over the side, and Marty once again scrambled up. This time he carried a briefcase, making the climb awkward.

The captain met him at the rail and took the briefcase, allowing Marty to board the trawler. The two men fell into a deep discussion, and Sara could see Harry Yost listening from the deck of the fishing boat below.

As she watched the men on deck, she wondered what Harry was doing here. He and Nancy had had some hard times, especially after Harry got hurt last year. Still, this looked like a very bad way to catch up.

The captain opened the briefcase and inspected the contents, much as Marty had inspected the large suitcase earlier. A flash of anger crossed his face. He slammed the briefcase closed, and shoved it back at Marty, with a shout.

Marty retreated to the rail of the trawler, dropping the brief-case at his feet. He held a hand out in supplication, as though try-ing to appease the captain. The captain clasped his hands behind his back and stared hard at Marty, then looked down at Harry on the deck below.

Marty said something more, and the captain looked back at him. Even with the poor spyglass, Sara could see Marty sweating, in spite of the chill. The trawler crew had disappeared into the wheelhouse, leaving just Marty and the captain on deck.

The captain spoke again, and Marty answered, hope flashing briefly across his face. The captain's harsh reply made him jump, and he knocked the briefcase over the side. It landed on the deck of the *Janice Lee,* where Harry grabbed it.

Sara eased the window open, and rested her glass against the broad sill. The captain stood unmoving, as the trawler rocked in a small swell, and Marty clutched at the rail. He answered the captain.

Matt's voice, slurred with sleep, whispered from the bunk. "What's going on?"

Without taking her eye from the glass she whispered back. "Marty's back. He's on board the trawler. Looks like he and the Russian captain are arguing over something."

Although Sara couldn't hear Marty's words, she saw him shrug as though denying his fear. It didn't convince her, but the cap-tain's face softened, and he stepped closer to Marty, clapping one large hand on Marty's shoulder.

She heard Matt slide down from the bunk, his bare feet making a small slapping noise as they hit the worn linoleum of the floor.

"Matt, do you have any idea why Harry is — "

The captain's movement was swift and sure, like the strike of a coiled snake. The gun registered in her brain, and the sharp report of a single shot cut off her words, forcing a scream of ter-ror from her throat.

Chapter 19

Sara's scream went through Matt like a knife, cutting away the cobwebs of sleep and sending adrenaline surging through his veins. He reached her in one long stride. Clapping a hand across her mouth, he pulled Sara away from the window, straining to see the cause of her scream.

Across the bay, men were scrambling around the decks of both boats. Marty was sprawled over the side of the trawler, his head lolling at an impossible angle, blood dripping down the remains of his forehead into the water.

The trawler captain shouted at Harry, who shook his head wildly and waved his arms. The crew poured out of the trawler's wheelhouse in response to a shouted command, and Matt heard the engines begin to speed up.

"Come on!" Matt hissed, trying to keep his voice low. He didn't stop for shoes, but swung up the ladder, two rungs at a time. He trusted that Sara would follow. He needed her.

Their only hope was to run, before the crews of the trawler and *Janice Lee* could throw off the lines that held the boats together. They were out of range of the gun he had seen in the captain's hand, but there was no way to know what other weapons might be on board.

Sara appeared at the top of the ladder. Matt caught a brief glimpse of her ashen face as a spotlight from across the bay illuminated the wheelhouse of *Excelsior*. She was terrified, but he couldn't stop to reassure her.

"While I start the engines, I want you to cut the anchor rope, and then high-tail it back here and hang on."

He thrust a heavy knife into her hands, its razor-sharp blade still guarded by a leather sheath. The click of the latch as she opened the door was as loud as an explosion to Matt's ears, but silence no longer mattered, only speed.

Matt set his mouth in a single, grim line, and reached for the starter. The grinding of the starter sounded as loud as a freight train in the tiny wheelhouse. For one heart-stopping second, the engines refused to turn over. Matt gritted his teeth, drew a deep breath, reset the choke and pushed the starter button again.

This time the engines roared to life, the sound loud and reassuring. He ran the engines up, wishing he had time to warm them up properly.

Peering back over his shoulder, he saw Sara, caught in the beam of a spotlight, raise her arm high over her head, and swing it in a long arc. Even with the engines throbbing, he heard the ringing of the blade as it hit the gunwale.

Sara stepped back, stowing the knife, and turned for the wheelhouse. Matt took his cue and threw *Excelsior* into gear. He prayed that Sara was securely fastened to the jack line, in case she lost her footing as he powered toward the narrow mouth of the bay. He didn't have time to look, he had to trust her, but the need to reassure himself was like a crushing weight.

Unable to stop himself, he tore his eyes from the charts and the water, and glanced over his shoulder. He saw a dark shape moving along the midline of the ship. He didn't stop to focus, just caught the movement as he turned his head, and went back to the water ahead of him. Sara could take care of herself.

Over the roar of the diesels, he heard a shout from the direction of the trawler. Matt couldn't look. He didn't have to. He knew they would soon be after him - after them.

The door to the wheelhouse banged open and Sara staggered into the tiny space. "It's cut," she said, her breath ragged.

Matt didn't turn his head, just nodded. He was focused on the narrow passage rushing at him. The channel was tricky, even with a flooding tide, and right now the tide was low. He kept the running lights off, depending on his antiquated instruments to show him where he was.

"We'd have been stood on end by now if it wasn't," he answered. "Good job." He wanted to hug her, congratulate her on a job well done, but he couldn't take his attention from the helm.

"What's going on over there?" Matt nodded toward the trawler, never moving his eyes from the water. They were in the mouth of the bay now, the ancient depth finder pinging wildly as they crossed the shallow bar that protected the bay.

They slid past the bar, and the pinging slowed as the bottom dropped away. They had made it this far. They were in the open ocean.

So far, so good. But which way should he go from here?

Chapter 20

Sara looked behind them as Matt steered *Excelsior* out of the bay. She clenched her hands into fists, willing the boat to go faster, to speed them away from the dangers of smugglers with guns. Although Sara had seen only the captain with a gun, she imagined that all the crew might have guns, or have access to them.

The boat heeled over as Matt cleared the mouth of the bay and turned south. They were flying over the water, her view of the trawler and the fishing boat obscured for fleeting moments by the forest on the southern arm of the bay. She craned her neck as the boat skipped over the breakers, watching the other boats as best she could.

Her view was obscured by a clump of trees, then she saw them again. "Now they're running around. One of them is at the anchor winch." More trees. It was like watching a jerky, old-time movie, the characters jumping from one place to another with each frame she saw. "They're free of the *Janice Lee,* but Harry's just standing there. No, wait. He's pulling away." She watched the two boats separate.

"The Russians are weighing anchor." She could see the anchor spool begin to turn, wet rope curling around the giant spindle. Then they were lost from sight again.

Sara's clenched hands were jammed in the pockets of her jeans. She could feel each hard knuckle pressing into her thighs, and the stubby nails were beginning to dig into her palms.

"Is there anything I can do to help? I can't really see anything more through the trees at this point."

Matt shook his head. "Not really, except keep a lookout for them coming out of the bay. I figure we've got a couple minutes while they get organized." He paused to flip on the tiny chart light, stare at the charts spread across the table, and glance at the GPS.

"Can you grab me a soda? I could use the caffeine."

Sara dropped down the ladder, glad of something to do. She snagged two cans from the cooler, then hollered up at Matt. "Would you rather have coffee? I could start it."

"Yes, but no. There isn't time. I need you back up here."

She scuttled back up the ladder, the cold cans clutched in one hand as she climbed with the other. She popped the tops, and handed a can to Matt, who drained half the can in a single, open-throated chug.

"Keep a watch out the stern," Matt said, without looking at her. "Let me know the minute you see any sign of them."

Matt steered the boat through more breakers, keeping close to the rocky outcroppings of the shore. He had doused the chart light, and continued to check the GPS and depth finder.

He was looking for something, but he didn't slow down. He kept *Excelsior* running at top speed, crashing through the breakers with bone-jarring drops over the top. The ride was as wild as the height of the storm, but without the waves crashing over them.

"Now we call," Matt said. He waved at the radio. "Hand me the mike."

At last! Help would come soon, and the waiting and running would be over. Sara was already feeling relieved.

"Shit!" Matt cursed, and threw the microphone down. It dangled at the end of its spiraled cord, bobbing with the rocking of the boat. "Radio's not working."

"But it was fine when you talked to Josh yesterday."

"That was yesterday." Matt's voice was grim. "We've been bounced around some since then. Probably just something knocked loose, but I don't have time to look for the problem right now."

The one thing Matt had not said was that she had piloted the boat since then. Sara worried that she had done something to damage the radio. Her stomach knotting with fear and guilt, she turned her attention to the boats behind them.

"Is there some way I can help?" she asked over her shoulder. She couldn't look at Matt, knowing it could be her fault.

Matt hesitated, then his shoulders slumped in resignation. He pointed to the emergency beacon mounted on the far corner of the helm.

"Trigger it."

Sara pushed the activation button, but nothing happened. "Is that all?" she asked.

The answer was a swift string of profanities.

"No. It's supposed to beep and flash."

She pushed the button again. Nothing.

"Can we do anything?"

"No, not right now. We can check it when we stop."

She saw the bulky form of the trawler, outlined in lights, emerge from Pelican Bay, its spotlight searching the channel in the gloom. They seemed to be moving very slowly, carefully picking their way across the low bar that the smaller *Excelsior* had taken at high speed.

The trawler reached open water, and stopped. Sara's heart leapt, beating wildly. *Excelsior* was running without lights. Maybe the trawler couldn't see which way they had gone.

Hope replaced the fear for a moment, but it was short-lived. Her moment of relief shattered, sending jagged shards through her veins, as the reality of their situation sunk in. They were alone on the open ocean, a trawler full of smugglers was looking for them, and the engines were throbbing at full volume. And who knew what Harry and the crew of the *Janice Lee* would do.

"They can't see where we are!" she shouted to Matt. "But can't they hear us?"

Matt shrugged, his attention on the water. "Sound carries differently out here. They can hear us, but they can't be sure where the sound is coming from in the dark." He flipped on the chart light, indicating the chart on the table, and Sara looked where he was pointing. "They should expect us to go north, looking for the closest port where we can get help."

She could see what he was saying. There was what appeared to be a large port much closer in that direction. "So why are we going south?"

"One, because that isn't what they'll expect." Matt shut off the chart light. "And, two, because I think I know a place where we can hide. If they don't catch us." Matt emptied the soda can and wiped his mouth on his sleeve.

Sara turned back to watch behind them, her heart racing. She couldn't seem to catch her breath, her body demanding larger and larger quantities of oxygen. She drew one fast, quivering breath after another, almost panting. She could feel her head swimming, and her vision blurred.

The slap took her by surprise, Matt's open hand striking her cheek with a sharp crack. "Don't do that!" he yelled.

"You hit me!" Sara didn't know whether to cry, scream, or hit him back. His words registered, and she yelled back, "Do what?"

"Hyperventilate. I need you here, not passed out on the floor." His attention was back on the water.

"I'm sorry," he said, regret clear in his voice, "but I had to do that. It was the fastest way to snap you out of it. I'd rather have you pissed off than passed out."

The tone of his voice told her how difficult it must have been for him. Never, in all their years together, had he raised a hand to her. Her anger melted, and she instantly forgave him. He was a gentle man by nature, and it must have hurt him a lot.

They were well away from the bay now, hugging the rocky shoreline as close as Matt dared. She watched the trawler turn. Time slowed to a crawl, and the trawler seemed to hang suspended for endless minutes. Sara held her breath, as the trawler swung about, her bow pointed north, and hope exploded again.

"They're turning north! They're turning north! Oh, Matt, you're a genius!" She was giddy with relief, bouncing on her toes, her hands clapping with her joy.

"Then we might have a few minutes before they decide we're not out there." Matt's assessment sent her plummeting into despair once again. "But that should be enough time to reach Tunnel Island."

Sara threw her arms around Matt's broad back and hugged herself to him. She had no idea where or what Tunnel Island was, but Matt thought they would be safe there until they could get help — and right now all she wanted was to be safe from the trawler, the battling sailors, and the captain and his huge gun.

"Keep a close watch. If they haven't caught us in the next fifteen minutes, we should be safe."

Sara nodded and looked at her watch. She stared hard behind them, then realized she could be using the good binoculars that were stored in the wheelhouse. In their mad dash from the bay, she had forgotten about them.

She raised the binoculars to her eyes, and suddenly the trawler was in view again. She could read the name on the stern with ease. *Ludmilla*. They were Russian, as Matt had suspected. The boat was moving steadily north, and Sara watched with growing hope as she grew smaller in the distance.

Nothing else moved on the water, and Sara wondered where Harry and the *Janice Lee* were. Since she hadn't seen them emerge, they must be in Pelican Bay, trying to recover from Marty's shooting.

Ten minutes passed. Eleven. Twelve.

The wheelhouse was silent, except for the steady throb of *Excelsior*'s engines. Sara"s heart was fluttering. Her mood grew lighter with each passing minute. She checked her watch again. Twelve and a half minutes. She watched the hand sweep around, measuring another thirty seconds, then sixty. A minute and a half. Then they would be safe, as Matt had promised.

Her hopes soared. One more minute. Maybe, if their luck held, they could just keep going all the way to Gray's Harbor, and the docks of Westport. They could empty the hold, get a hot meal, and head home.

She could just make out a figure standing in the stern of the trawler. She caught the glint of light on glass as the man on the trawler turned. She realized with a growing sense of horror that he was standing on deck holding a pair of binoculars pointed in the direction of *Excelsior*.

The man dropped the glasses, letting them hang around his neck. He moved nimbly toward the cabin of the trawler. She didn't know if he had seen them or not.

Of course he couldn't see them. Even though the first hint of dawn was beginning to lighten the sky, it was dark. They had shown no lights, except the few brief seconds when Matt had turned on the dim chart lights. It was impossible to think they had been seen. But maybe the Russians had some high-tech gadget that let them see in the dark. Sara had seen things like that on TV.

Her blood ran cold as she watched the distant lights of *Ludmilla* waver. Was she turning, or had she stopped? Maybe the man with the binoculars had seen nothing, and they were giving up the chase and heading for home.

But the roller coaster ride wasn't over yet. Sara plunged down another steep drop as she watched the trawler come about. They must have been seen.

"Oh, God!" Sara was near tears. The stress of the almost sleepless night and then the constant cycle of hope and despair had pushed her close to the breaking point.

"What?" Matt yelled over the throbbing engines. He didn't look back, keeping his attention on their course.

"They turned around." Sara swallowed hard, trying to control her fear and rising panic. "I think they saw us."

"Hang on."

The boat cut sharply toward the shoreline. Sara continued to watch *Ludmilla* through the binoculars. The captain was on deck now, moving into the pulpit at the bow. He had a glass in his hand, which he raised to his eye.

"Here we go," Matt called.

Sara turned to look forward. In front of them was a small, rocky island. The ocean funneled through a narrow passage on the landward side of the island, and they were headed for that passage. It looked far too small for *Excelsior,* but the determined set of Matt's jaw told her there must be room.

The trawler was still headed their direction when they plunged through the choppy water into the relative calm of a small cove. Ahead, Sara could see another section of chop where the cove once again met the open ocean, at the far side of the island.

The trawler was no longer visible, blocked by the rocky cliffs of the island rising behind them. Matt quickly cut the engines back, and reached for the radio.

"Now," he said, "we figure out how to fix this, and call out the cavalry."

Chapter 21

Matt glanced at Sara in the faint glow of the chart light. Her face was pale, the binoculars still clutched in her hands. Her knuckles were white with the force of her grip.

"I can fix it," he said. "But I need time. Come here." He gestured at the chart spread on the table.

"There isn't much room in here, and that trawler won't be able to come into the cove. But they might figure out where we are." He took the binoculars from her and hung them up. He held her hand tight, and looked into her eyes. There was fear there, but he could see the strength underneath.

"You're going to take the wheel and be my lookout, while I work on the radio. If there is any sign of that trawler, or any hint that they've found us, run up the engines and head out. I'll take over, but we can't waste a second if we're spotted."

Sara nodded, her eyes as big as dinner plates. Matt bent and kissed her gently.

He could see the faint touch of pink in the shape of a hand, across her cheek. Tears of shame stung the back of his eyes, and he blinked them away. It had been an emergency, but he would carry the guilt of that slap for a long time.

Sara returned the kiss. They lingered for a moment, clinging to each other, and to the illusion of normalcy. Then Matt pulled away, and Sara took the wheel.

Matt scrambled through the tool locker, digging out a flashlight and the small hand tools he would need to tackle the radio.

It was probably something minor. Please, God, he prayed silently, let it be something minor.

He reached for the mike, returning it to its proper place in the holster on the side of the radio. He checked over the settings, making sure the power was turned on and the channel was properly selected.

He could feel the stiffness in Sara's posture next to him. Her muscles were taut with strain, and he could almost hear the churning of her stomach. But she seemed more under control than she had been earlier. He longed to hold her close and tell her how he admired her courage and determination, but there was no time.

"Doing fine," he murmured as he fiddled with the radio settings.

"What?" It was Sara's turn to speak without looking, as he had done earlier.

I just said you're doing fine," he answered. He checked the various connectors, making sure nothing had been knocked loose in their wild ride. They seemed secure. He was rapidly running out of minor problems.

Matt loosened the brackets that held the radio against the wall, and tilted the receiver forward. There were a couple permanent connectors on the back of the unit.

There was the problem. Sometime in the last day, since he had last used the radio, the connector had broken loose from the wire that fed from the antenna, high overhead. All he had to do was fix the connector and reconnect the radio to the antenna.

Matt fumbled with the connector, cutting the broken end of the wire and fashioning an awkward splice. He reconnected everything, and keyed the mike. Nothing.

"I saw something," Sara said.

"What?" Matt had his head craned over the back of the radio. He couldn't see anything but the narrow vision of the various wires and connectors.

"A boat passed the northern entrance. I think it may have been *Ludmilla*."

"Who in the hell is Ludmilla?" Matt was trying once more to connect the antenna wire. He really didn't care about Ludmilla, whoever she was.

"Not who," Sara said. "What. *Ludmilla* is the name of the trawler. Russian, just like you thought." To Matt's surprise, she was keeping her voice steady.

"Okay. Which way was she heading?"

He had the wires connected to the plug again. It wasn't pretty, but it might work.

"Headed south."

"Okay. Keep watching."

Sara laid a soft hand against his back, as though she was trying to reassure him. "Sure, honey."

Matt twisted the antenna wire back into position, replugged all the connections, and turned on the power. Still he heard nothing.

He set the radio to scan, hoping to pick up a transmission. If he heard something, anything, he would know the antenna was working again.

The tuner scanned through the frequencies, each one displayed in large red numbers on the face of the radio. Still, silence filled the cabin, while the powerful diesels continued their throbbing.

Now Matt was the one having trouble catching his breath. He closed his eyes for a few seconds as the frequency number changed, and forced slow, even breaths in through his nose and out through his mouth. His breathing settled into a more normal rhythm, and he opened his eyes.

The radio squawked to life suddenly, causing Matt to jump. His heart was racing madly, but he was jubilant. He had fixed the radio! Now they could call the Coast Guard, and get this all behind them. He'd worry about the emergency beacon later.

But the Coast Guard would ask their location. They always did. It was routine. If he told them, he would be telling the world — a world that included the trawler, *Ludmilla*.

He would have to lie. It wasn't something he would have imagined doing, but then he had never imagined taking Sara with him on a trip, or finding smugglers in a tiny bay on the Washington Peninsula, or being chased by men with guns. Lying to the Coast Guard would be another first.

The squawking continued, and Matt fiddled with the tuning.

All at once, a voice boomed clearly from the radio in mid-sentence.

" ... don't see them. You sure they aren't farther north?"

A chunk of ice formed in the pit of Matt's stomach. The voice was Harry Yost of the *Janice Lee*.

A heavily accented voice answered Harry. "I am sure." The man's English sounded formal and stilted, as though he had learned to speak English in a classroom, or from a book. "They were not visible, and we should have overtaken them. One of my men thought he had seen them to the south of us. That is why we returned this way."

"Well, we sure as hell didn't see them."

"You must continue to look," the foreign voice said. "We must assure ourselves of a good catch."

It could only be the captain of the trawler. Matt was sure what catch he referred to, and he wasn't after the fish in Matt's hold.

"Yeah." Harry's voice was tight, wavering. "Whatever you say. But I'm telling you, they aren't down here, and I need to finish my catch, and get it to the processor. Today."

"You should reach our position within fifteen minutes," the captain replied. "We will discuss further efforts at that time."

The click as the captain ended his transmission elicited a string of profanities from Harry, but there was no one to hear them except Matt and Sara — and whoever else might be using that frequency. But to anyone else, it would have sounded like a disagreement between boats of a fleet, not a search for witnesses.

"Matt!" Sara's voice was tight, strangled in her throat.

"It's okay, honey," he lied. "We can call the Coast Guard. The radio's fixed. Then we run north, sell the fish, and," he glanced wistfully at the stern, "buy a new anchor."

"Then can we go home?" Sara asked in a small voice.

"Sure." Matt knew they would have to fish on the way home, and get back to Newport with the holds full, to make up for the extra fuel and the loss of their anchor. But this wasn't the time to explain that to Sara.

He turned to channel 16, and keyed the mike.

"Pan-pan, pan-pan, pan-pan. Coast Guard station *Astoria*, this is the vessel *Excelsior* calling. Repeat, this is the vessel *Excelsior*. Over."

The radio crackled to life immediately, and Matt reached to readjust the squelch. "*Excelsior*, this is Coast Guard station *Astoria*. Switch and answer channel two-two alpha, two-two alpha. Over."

"Coast Guard, this is *Excelsior*, switching to two-two alpha." Matt hoped the trawler and *Janice Lee* were still on the other channel, and hadn't heard the call. But he couldn't be sure. He would have to lie.

Matt quickly changed the radio frequency, and called again. The Coast Guard operator answered immediately.

"*Excelsior,* Coast Guard. What is the emergency?"

"Coast Guard, about ninety minutes ago we observed some suspicious activity in Pelican Bay. We believe contraband was exchanged. We were able to elude the trawler involved, but we believe they are pursuing us. Over."

"Roger, *Excelsior.* What is your present location?"

"South of Tunnel Island, about fifteen miles."

"That's wrong," Sara said, as he released the mike button. "We're right next to the island."

"Yeah. Do you want to tell that Russian captain where we are? I'll apologize to the Coast Guard later. Right now, I don't want to tell anyone where we are."

He turned his attention back to the radio.

"Can you see the pursuing vessel?"

"Not now. But we could up to a couple minutes ago."

"Roger. We've launched a search team. Can you describe the vessel?"

"Trawler, probably 70-feet or so. Wheelhouse amidships. Coast Guard, my wife says she saw the name on the stern. That vessel is *Ludmilla,* like the woman's name. Over."

"Say again, *Excelsior.*"

"The trawler is named *Ludmilla.* It's a woman's name."

"Roger, *Excelsior.* How about the other vessels involved?"

Matt paused. This was the question he had been worried about. He didn't want to tell them about Harry, and he had already told one lie, what would another one matter?

"One unidentified fishing vessel. Still in the bay, last we saw of her."

Matt motioned Sara aside and took the helm. He had done all he could.

"Roger that. Can you give us any description of the other vessel?"

Matt reached up and loosened the mike plug as he ran the engines up. Sara looked at him with a question in her eyes.

"It's time to go. There's the very real chance that Harry or the trawler heard part of that."

The Coast Guard was repeating the question when Matt keyed the mike with the loose connection. He mumbled a reply that didn't have any actual words, and jiggled the plug, hoping he was creating a mass of static on the receiving end. Let them think he was having radio troubles. It wouldn't be far from wrong.

"*Excelsior. Excelsior.* This is Coast Guard *Astoria.* You're breaking up. Please try again."

Matt reconnected the mike plug, but he ignored the call. He brought *Excelsior* around, her bow facing north, and began the nerve-wracking process of guiding her through the channel, back into the open ocean.

Chapter 22

Sara watched as Matt guided them through the rough waters of the channel. She knew the currents were tricky, and it took all of Matt's concentration to keep *Excelsior* in the navigable part of the passage.

Sheltered by the island, they hadn't felt the rising wind that came in with the faint morning light. As soon as they cleared the island, though, they heeled over as the force of the wind hit them.

Sara was holding onto the chart table bracing herself for the wild ride through the passage. But Matt was more relaxed. Caught off guard, he was thrown sideways and one foot went out from under him. His weight landed heavily on the other foot, and Sara heard a sickening crunch.

Unable to support himself, Matt dropped to the floor of the wheelhouse. His hands were torn loose from the wheel, and *Excelsior* was running at full speed without a pilot.

Matt didn't seem able to get back up.

Sara didn't have time to think. She grabbed the wheel, fighting for control. Her muscles strained as she battled to bring her about. Slowly, they turned into the wind, and the violent pitching settled into a steady roll.

Sara carefully began turning again, setting the northerly course she had watched Matt plot. She knew more or less where they were going, now that the boat was back under control.

Matt still hadn't moved. Sara heard a faint moan as he tried to get his feet under him. She quickly engaged the autopilot, and prayed that her course was somewhere near correct.

A quick glance behind her showed no sign of *Ludmilla,* or *Janice Lee.* With luck, they were now many miles south, and in the path of the approaching Coast Guard. She could worry about them later. Right now, her number one concern was her husband.

With a last look at the autopilot settings, Sara knelt at Matt's side. His face was twisted with pain and there was a pallor beneath his tan. He opened his eyes, and tried to smooth the pain lines from his face.

"I think I just twisted it," he said, waving a hand at his ankle. "Thanks for taking the helm. Give me a minute to catch my breath, and I'll get back up."

Sara looked at the pain in his eyes. "Like hell you will." She reached for a life vest to use as a cushion, and helped Matt prop himself against the wall of the cabin. "You'll stay put for at least a few minutes, until we're sure how bad this is."

Sara left Matt propped against the wall, and rushed out on deck. She grabbed a bucket normally used for cleaning the deck, and opened the hold. Below her lay hundreds, no, thousands, of fish, on a bed of ice.

She lay down on the deck, and dangled the bucket into the hold. Digging under the fish with her hands, she reached the layer of ice. She began to scoop chunks of ice into the bucket. Her bare hands chilled quickly, but she kept digging and scooping, gathering a few chunks at a time in her frozen fingers, until the bucket was nearly full.

Slamming the hatch shut, she lugged the bucket of ice back into the cabin. In the few minutes she had been gone, Matt had managed to hike up his pant leg, exposing the ankle that was already swelling. Blotches of blue and purple marked Matt's ankle, with bright red streaks running just under the skin of his foot, to disappear in his deck shoe. If it was only a sprain, it was a nasty one.

Looking at Matt's injured ankle made her stomach hollow, and little icicles of fear shot through her veins. But there wasn't time to be squeamish. She took a deep breath and looked away until she could control her stomach.

She could see that the ankle was badly injured. Twisted, sprained, broken, it didn't matter. Matt wasn't going to do much for a while. It would be up to her to take care of both of them. She took another deep breath, set her jaw, and went to work.

She removed Matt's jeans, so they wouldn't have to be cut off if the swelling got worse. She filled a towel with the chunks of ice, smashing the bundle against the deck to break up the larger pieces, and wrapped the ice pack around Matt's ankle. Digging in the first aid box, she uncovered two codeine painkillers left over from Matt's last accident. She gave them to him with a glass of water. It was the best she could do.

There was an elastic bandage, but Sara was uneasy about trying to wrap the ankle. If they could control the swelling first, it might be easier to bandage it.

Matt swallowed the painkillers without protest, but he was already getting restless.

"I can get up," he insisted. As if to prove it, he dragged himself to the wheel. Using his uninjured leg, he pulled himself upright. But just standing made him gasp in pain, and drained the tiny amount of returning color from his face.

Sara grabbed a folding stool from beneath the chart table, and slid it under Matt. The stool was too low for him to see over the windowsills easily, but sitting up seemed to calm him. He let Sara put the ice pack back on his ankle, and he sat still while she checked their course and adjusted the autopilot.

"I need to check the charts," Matt said through gritted teeth. "I have to be sure we're on course."

He tried to stand, but quickly dropped back onto the stool with a hiss of pain.

"I would suggest you don't do that," Sara said dryly. "It might hurt."

Chapter 23

The sarcastic tone took Matt by surprise. He stared at Sara for a few seconds, then began to laugh.

But he needed to check those charts.

"Help me to the chart table, would you?"

Sara's look was skeptical, but she relented, scooting the stool while he hung on to whatever he could reach to steady himself. After a couple minutes of scooting and shoving, Matt was in position to read the charts.

"I know," Matt replied. "But I like to check it against the charts. Besides, there are things on these charts that aren't on the GPS."

"Oh? Like what?"

"Well..." Matt hesitated. There really wasn't anything specific, just the years of experience that made using the charts second nature to him. "Just things. Marks that I put there, things I know, places I've been."

Sara just looked at him, then pointedly turned to check their heading on the GPS.

Matt stared at the charts, trying to make sense of them. His ankle hurt like hell, and the effort of moving, even a few feet, had left him weaker and more shaken than he wanted to admit. He believed it was just a sprain, but he knew it was a bad one. The pain of moving had carved a hollow in his stomach, and his head was swimming.

With an enormous effort, Matt managed to get control of his head and his stomach. The painkillers would kick in soon, the ice was beginning to numb the ankle, and he promised himself that soon he would be able to move.

They were plowing north, occasional gusts of wind pushing hard against them, as the eastern sky grew lighter with the coming dawn. The hold was full and they had a good payday ahead of them. The Coast Guard should be looking for Harry and Russians. In a few hours they would be home free.

Matt relaxed, letting himself sag against the chart table. He rested his arms on the table, and lay his head on his folded arms. He would just rest here for a few minutes, just until the painkillers kicked in. Then he could take the helm, and pilot the *Excelsior* to La Push.

He just needed to rest for a minute first.

Just until his ankle stopped throbbing so much.

● ● ●

The engines changed pitch, and Sara's voice penetrated his sleep-fogged brain.

"Matt! Matt! Wake up, Matt!" There was an edge of hysteria in her voice that jerked him to attention. The sudden movement sent pain knifing through his leg, and adrenaline washed through him.

"What? What is it?" Matt was disoriented, and it took a few seconds to realize he was sitting in front of the chart table. In that instant, he remembered what had happened, and he knew he had fallen asleep, when he only meant to rest his head for a few minutes.

"I saw something, Matt. I think there's a boat behind us."

"It's a big ocean, honey. There are lots of boats. There's no reason to get so upset. Besides, the Coast Guard should have those guys in custody by now. It's probably nothing."

But Matt's heart was racing from the adrenaline rush, and he couldn't relax again until he assured himself and Sara that there was nothing to worry about.

Stretching out his arm, Matt snagged the binoculars that Sara had hung back in place. He placed them to his eyes, straining to see through the back window. Grunting with frustration, he pushed himself up on his good foot, keeping the other firmly braced on the ice pack.

Matt got the binoculars pointed in the right direction, and swung them in a slow arc across the ocean behind them. At first, he couldn't see anything. Sara had over-reacted. There wasn't anything out there.

"I don't see anything. Are you sure - " Matt froze in mid-sentence. "Oh, shit!"

"I was right."

"Looks like it." Matt dropped the binoculars, looked at the chart to check their position, and turned back to Sara. "Thanks for the help," he said, nudging her away from the wheel with his hip.

He grabbed the wheel, resting his bad leg on the stool, taking the weight on his knee and letting the foot hang over the side. It still throbbed, but the worst of the lightheadedness had passed. He released the autopilot. He could pilot *Excelsior*, though he wasn't sure where he was headed.

He just knew it had to be someplace where the trawler wouldn't, or couldn't, follow.

But this time he wouldn't wait to call for help.

When Matt picked up the mike and keyed the button, nothing happened. He could still hear the static of the empty channel on the receiver. His heart sank. First the antenna, now the mike. He was afraid to think about what might be next.

Matt gritted his teeth against the pain in his ankle, and clutched the wheel. He focused on the chart, on the throbbing of *Excelsior*'s engines, on anything but his foot.

The morning sun was shining off the water, and Matt had to squint to see where he was going. He grabbed his sunglasses from the rack above his head and shoved them on his face. It helped a little.

"Take the binoculars."

● ● ●

Sara grabbed the binoculars from where he had dropped them. Without being told, she raised them to her eyes and scanned for the trawler behind them.

She could see it, not much more than a speck on the horizon, but the silhouette was definitely a trawler. The question was whether it was "their" trawler.

The trawler was a faster boat, with more powerful engines. There was no question that it could overtake them. The only question was how long would it take.

Sara heard and felt the change as Matt pushed the diesels to the max. They were running as fast as they could, but the trawler was gaining on them with each passing minute.

Matt bent over the charts, as if searching for something. Sara heard a grunt of satisfaction, and glanced back to see him plotting a new course. But she was the lookout, and it was her job to keep watch. She went back to the binoculars.

The trawler was closer, but she couldn't tell if it was *Ludmilla* or not. She couldn't keep her heart from racing at the thought, but she could control her other reactions. She forced slow breaths through her lungs, and resisted the urge to clench her hands into fists. She would remain calm.

"There it is!" Matt's voice was exultant. He steered *Excelsior* through the surf, toward the shore. All Sara could see was a narrow strip of beach between low, rocky cliffs. Surely Matt didn't intend to ground them in an attempt to escape the trawler. Especially now that he couldn't walk. They would be sitting ducks.

As they drew nearer the cliffs, Sara found it harder and harder to control her breathing. It threatened to turn into terror-driven panting. She clamped her lips together, holding them with her teeth. Forced to breathe through her nose, she began to regain control.

Closer to the cliffs, Sara could see that there were small gaps all along the faces. Water ran through some of them, and hardy madrone trees clung to the top of the rocks, their gnarled branches bent inland by the constant wind. They looked desolate and forbidding. Sara could take no comfort from the shoreline.

Sara forced herself to look back through the binoculars, trying to ignore the cliff face rushing at them.

With a sudden movement, Matt pulled *Excelsior* toward the shore. They rode up the back of a swell, and crashed over the top.

Sara stared through the binoculars at the trawler. She was scared of the trawler, but even more afraid to look at where Matt was taking them. The boat was distant, but she could see that it was gaining by the minute. She had to hope that Matt knew what he was doing.

Excelsior crashed through another swell, and this time Sara couldn't help herself; she had to look. To her amazement, a narrow channel had opened in front of them, little more than a slit in the rocky face of the cliff. She could see through the slit, to where a small river rushed to join the ocean. She understood what Matt was doing, finding a place where the trawler couldn't follow.

But it was so tight, she wasn't sure they could even get *Excelsior* into the mouth of the river. Matt's entire attention was absorbed in piloting the boat, his face a mask of concentration. Flashes of pain crossed his face each time they took a jolt, but he didn't seem to notice. His hands were clenched on the wheel, his eyes staring at the water, reading it the way other people read a road map.

He reached for the throttle, cutting power to the engines, slowing for the approach to the cut. He carefully turned the boat and guided her through the tiny passage. Sara held her breath as they passed between the rocky cliffs. It felt like they were so close, she could reach out and touch them.

"Are they back there?"

Matt's voice brought Sara's attention back to the trawler that had been following them.

"I don't see anything. Yet."

Sara peered through the binoculars at the narrow strip of ocean that was visible between the cliffs, while Matt maneuvered *Excelsior*. Silent minutes crawled past as they waited for the trawler to show itself. The tension was a thick blanket, holding them motionless as they watched and waited.

After long minutes, a trawler passed the mouth of the river, her diesels echoing faintly across the water. Sara couldn't see the name on the transom, but she could hear Matt's sigh of relief. It wasn't *Ludmilla*.

"Well, I feel really foolish now," Sara said, her voice quaking with relief. "All that for nothing."

"It wasn't for nothing. At this point I'm a true believer in "better safe than sorry"."

Matt's voice was strained. Sara turned. His face was pasty. Deep lines of pain bracketed his mouth, and he seemed to sway a little where he stood. He didn't say anything more, just lowered himself onto the stool.

Chapter 24

Sara reached his side in a single step. She put her arms around him, and felt his weight sag against her. The flight had taken more out of him than he had to give, and he was near collapse.

Supporting him with her body, Sara turned Matt around so that he could lean over the chart table, where he had napped earlier. The diesels were still running at idle, and *Excelsior* was drifting in the current of the river. She would have to set the anchor and shut down the engines before she could care for Matt.

Anchor! There was no anchor. She had severed the anchor rope sometime in the dark hours of the early morning, somewhere in another lifetime. There had to be something else she could do. She couldn't let them drift, the current was too strong.

Sara tried to wrap her brain around the problem as she steadied the boat in the current. The river widened out just beyond where they were, forming a large, shallow pool. Maybe she could find a solution there.

When she reached the wide spot, she discovered it was even larger than she had thought. It was a small cove, hidden behind the stone cliffs and the wind-sculpted trees. The river rushed along one side, sending eddies swirling into the wide cut its passage had created.

Sara idled the engines back, slowing to almost a walking pace. She could hear the pinging of the depth finder, warning her that they were approaching a dangerous shallow, but she didn't know what else to do.

Moving at a crawl, she maneuvered *Excelsior* into the relative protection of the cove. There was room for her to bring the boat about, but little margin for error. One wrong move and they would be aground.

She felt a scrape along the port side as she swung the bow around. *Excelsior* listed slightly, and stalled. Sara held her breath, cranking the wheel hard to port, and goosing the engines just a little.

The boat shuddered, then all at once she broke loose. Sara grabbed the throttle, slowing the engines again to keep from shooting back into the current. She gritted her teeth and concentrated on making minute adjustments to the steering. It was a little like trying to parallel park a semi.

It was a delicate, touch and go operation, as she wrestled the boat into the stillest water she could find. It wasn't perfect, but she was satisfied with their position. She set the engines to idle, but she couldn't shut them down. She might need them in a hurry if *Excelsior* began to drift too far.

Sara walked the deck from bow to stern, down both sides, checking their location. About halfway down the port side, she saw what she had caught on — a few feet below the surface of the clear water was the top of a tree.

Sometime in the distant past, this cove had been part of the forest. One tree had withstood the relentless river, and now its remains lie hidden beneath the water. It wasn't perfect, but it was a better moorage than she could have hoped for.

Using the remains of the anchor rope, she fastened a crude lasso. She wasn't sure she had the strength left in her arms to throw the heavy anchor rope. She held the loop in both hands, twisted her body, and threw it like a Frisbee across the water.

She missed. The loop disappeared into the deep water. Gritting her teeth, Sara dragged the soggy line back into the boat, and tried again. This time she snagged a limb, but when she tried to tighten the loop around it, the branch broke, drifting out of sight. Tears of frustration stung at her eyes as she hauled the rope back into the boat.

Sara gathered the rope again, her arms shaking with fatigue. She had to do this, there wasn't anyone else. She twisted again, sucked in a deep breath, and sent the loop sailing.

The force of her throw threatened to throw Sara overboard. She hung across the gunwale, clutching the rail, her feet slipping against the deck, then gripping. Shaking, she stood up and looked at the rope. It formed a line from the deck to the submerged tree, and she could see that the loop had settled over a sturdy section of trunk. She quickly made the line fast to a cleat on the deck.

Excelsior rode the current to the end of the mooring rope, and stopped. They had a moorage.

Sara made her way back to the wheelhouse, tiny currents of strength seeping back into her muscles and bones. She had stopped shaking, but she needed another minute before she could face Matt. When she was sure she would not falter, she entered the wheelhouse and knelt down to look at Matt's injured ankle.

The ice may have kept the swelling down, but the ankle was puffed to twice its normal size. The sides of his foot strained over the edges of his slip-on deck shoes. Ugly bruises covered his foot and ankle.

Sara's stomach did flip-flops as she gingerly turned the foot, looking at the injured ankle. Matt didn't flinch, and Sara guessed he had passed out.

She wrapped the ankle with the elastic bandage. She hoped it would make it possible for Matt to move around a little. Matt was snoring, and Sara left him where he was. She would fix a place for him to rest before she tried to move him.

Out on deck, Sara shuffled gear aside to clear a flat space. She brought the cushion from the galley bench, and blankets and pillows from the bed. The sun was bright, and she tried to rig a blanket to shade a small section of the deck. She found a couple extra life vests, and used them as bolsters for the makeshift cot she had fashioned.

Then she went to get Matt.

Sara stared at the sleeping face of her husband. A dark stubble of beard covered the lower half of his face. Pain and exhaustion carved lines deep in his cheeks. She could see a faint suggestion of what he would look like as he got older. He had a good face, one that would weather well. If she could just get them out of this spot.

She bent over Matt, hugging herself to him. She kissed him on the cheek. The scratchy stubble stung her lips, and she could feel the heat of his body. She laid her hand on his forehead, trying to decide if he was running a fever.

His face was cool, his forehead dry. Perhaps it was just the warmth of the closed cabin in the morning sunshine, and her imagination.

Matt stirred at her touch, and she spoke his name.

"Let me help you, honey. You need to lie down."

"Wanna stay here," Matt mumbled. "No ladders right now. Fine here." He turned his head and hunched his shoulders.

"You'll make everything else hurt if you stay there. Come on. I've got a place for you to lie down on deck."

Matt continued to grumble, but he allowed Sara to put her shoulder under his arm and drag him to his feet. She braced herself to take his weight, and they shuffled across the deck.

Sara's stomach growled. They had eaten some cold biscuits and cheese before fleeing Pelican Bay, but that had been many hours ago. They needed food, and a plan. In that order.

"Stay put," she ordered Matt, and went below to see what she could find for them to eat.

Chapter 25

Sara returned with sandwiches and beer. Sitting on the impro- vised cot, Matt felt his stomach rumble. She set the food down, and he managed a smile. "I could eat my shoe," he said. "Thanks."

"I suppose you could. You can't wear it, after all." She smiled back. "Let's eat."

Matt ate two sandwiches, and vetoed a third. He was full, and feeling drowsy, but he couldn't afford to sleep any more.

"If you take leftovers below, I'll see about the radio."

Sara nodded. She pulled him up on his good foot. His ankle was better, but it couldn't take any weight. Leaning on Sara, he hobbled into the wheelhouse. He looked around, marveling that Sara had wedged *Excelsior* into the tiny cove. He couldn't have done much better himself.

Sara came up and put her arms around him as he inspected the radio. Matt turned and kissed her. She smelled of sleep and sun. She tasted like mustard and beer. She'd moored the boat as well as any veteran hand, and she was the perfect woman.

Sara's arms tightened around his neck, and the kiss deepened. For the first time all day, he stopped for a minute and enjoyed the feeling of Sara in his arms.

"I did fix the beacon," he said. "The batteries were bad. It should have been serviced six months ago." Another expense he'd put off, and it had cost them a lot. "But the mike plug's fried. No spare, so we can't transmit. We ought to get out of here, and try for port tonight."

"No," Sara replied, her voice was firm. "You're hurt. You need rest. We can sell three-day-old fish. What we have is two days old. If you can't fix the radio go lie back down."

Matt tried to think of an argument. He couldn't. As he draped his arm over Sara's shoulder, he could feel where muscles were building, and she supported his weight better than he had expected, lowering him to the cushion. Now he knew he'd rather have her on board than Josh. Matt let go, let his body relax, and slid into a deep and dreamless sleep.

• • •

Sara split her time between watching Matt and watching the narrow strip of ocean visible between the cliffs. She couldn't use the radio, no one would hear her or *Excelsior* over the pounding of the surf against the rocks, and the passage was so shallow no one would expect a boat to pass through it. They were, for all intents, invisible.

She considered the emergency beacon. They could make port under their own power, and Matt's injury wasn't life threatening. This didn't justify the beacon.

So this was what fishing was really about. Out on the ocean alone, you depended on yourself, your boat, and your crew to get you home. And maybe you had to be lucky.

She'd sat with other wives, waiting for men whose luck had run out, and she had a newfound awareness of how fast it could happen. One bad choice or wrong move, and you didn't come home.

Long afternoon shadows covered the deck when Matt stirred. He reached a long arm across her legs, his hand on her hip. She felt drowsy, tempted to lie down and burrow into his embrace.

Instead, she wrenched away from Matt's touch, and checked the boat. The radio scanned, sputtering to life with bursts of distant traffic, and the instruments showed no change.

The sun slipped lower, and the sky faded to pale gray. It was near dusk when Matt propped up on one elbow, squinting up at her. "Why'd you let me sleep so long?"

"Could it be, um, because you needed to?"

Matt's hand snaked out and grabbed her ankle. "Come down here, woman. It hurts my neck to talk to you up there."

Sara yielded to his tugging, and settled next to him on the cushions. "How's the ankle?"

"Stiff. Sore. And about a thousand percent better." Matt patted her shoulder, and ran his fingers along her arm. He reached her hand and twined her fingers in his. They sat in silence, holding hands, and watching the sky grow darker.

Chapter 26

Anew moon was rising over the tops of the trees, and stars blanketed the sky, so thick Matt felt like he could reach up and grab a handful.

He pulled himself up, sitting with his arm around Sara. He watched her in silence for a few minutes, and felt the catch in her posture when she tried to move. The exertion of the last couple days was catching up with her muscles, more so now that the night air had cooled her body. He knew every muscle in her body must by aching.

Her shoulders were tight, and as he squeezed, a muffled groan announced that he had found one of the many sore muscles.

"You've taken care of me all day. Let me take care of you." Matt spread his legs, gingerly moving his swollen ankle, and pulled Sara back against him. He reached around her, grasped the bottom of her T-shirt, and pulled it over her head. As he suspected, the only thing underneath it was his wife. Sara started to protest, but Matt put a finger to her lips. "Just relax."

Her skin was warm. He put his hands back on her shoulders, and began to knead the knots of muscle he found. Her neck was a solid column, and he wrapped one strong hand around the back and worked it from side to side. He applied gentle pressure, forcing the muscles to stretch and flex.

Each time he pushed against her rigid muscles she would sigh or groan, and each time he could feel the cramped muscles give a little more than the last time. As her neck softened, he spread his attention to her shoulders. The flats of his palms pushed against the top of her back, and he dug hard fingers into the hollows of her collarbones.

Little by little, she began to respond to the massage. Her skin felt smooth, silky, under his hands, and her warm little bottom was pressed up against his crotch. The weak light of the new moon showed a faint outline of her body in front of him, but his memory filled in the rest. Firm breasts, long legs, and the tiny roundness of a soft, female belly. He didn't have to see these things to know they were there, and they stirred him.

Matt let go of Sara's shoulders and reached around her. With practiced ease, he unbuttoned her jeans and opened the zipper. Pulling her legs up, he slid the jeans and panties down. He ran his hands along her legs, pushing and rubbing at the muscles in her thighs and calves. She whimpered once, when he hit a particularly tightly knotted spot on her calf.

Reaching around to massage her legs like he did pressed Sara more tightly against Matt, and despite his injured ankle he could feel the growing heaviness in his groin. Each time she moved, she sent a little shiver of electricity through him. She would soon be aware of his reaction, if she wasn't yet.

Sara got up on her hands and knees, and turned to face Matt. As she did, her hand brushed against his crotch, making his stomach hollow. Her mouth formed a little "O" of surprise, and she smiled up at him.

"You're supposed to be resting."

"Well," he pulled her toward him. She rocked forward on her knees, and he kissed her. "Some parts don't seem to have gotten the message."

Matt ran his fingers along her collarbones, and up the sides of her neck, to hold her head as he kissed her again, harder and deeper. She reacted, her lips parting, returning the pressure.

He drew her closer, until her bare breasts brushed against his chest. He felt her nipples, already stiff from the evening chill, tighten further at the contact. He held her near, and continued his assault on her mouth.

Her breath caught in her throat, and Matt knew he was having an effect. He slid his hands from her head to her shoulders, and along her sides.

His hands stopped, spanning her slim waist, his fingers splayed against her back, thumbs on her rib cage. He could feel each breath she took, gauging the change in the rhythm as she drew a deep, shuddering breath. Her back arched, pressing her breasts to his chest, and her breath shuddered again.

The boat rocked on the water, pushing Sara against Matt. His hands gripped her waist, holding her close to him. He pulled back from her mouth, and lowered his head to her neck, kissing the hollow at the base of her throat. He could feel her pulse there, racing against the pressure of his lips. He nuzzled her neck, resting his head against her shoulder, and nipping at the soft skin below her jawline. She shuddered as his tongue and teeth roamed down her neck and along her collarbone.

"You really are supposed to be resting," Sara said. Pulling away from his touch, she stood over him, and glanced around her. Matt craned his neck to look up at her, her naked silhouette against the evening sky.

Sara glanced at his ankle, then stepped over him. She propped his foot on a pillow, with his other leg extended alongside. Then she stood straddling his legs and looked down at him.

"You really think you're ready to try this?"

Matt was staring at the dark thatch between her legs, inches in front of his face. His mouth went dry. He lay back and nodded, hoping she could see him in the dark.

Sara knelt down and sat back, her soft ass pressing against his knees. Matt put his hands on Sara's waist, sliding them over her hips, and reaching behind her to pinch her smooth bottom. He traced tiny circles with a fingertip at the base of her spine. It was a spot where Sara was extremely ticklish, but when she was aroused those spots became centers of great pleasure. She wiggled, moaning her approval. He slid his hand lower, one finger trailing along the depression that marked the first separation of her cheeks. That tickled her, too.

Sara scooted forward, leaning over and running her hands up Matt's body. As he tickled her back, her hands grabbed at him, fingertips digging into his skin. She lowered her head and ran her tongue across his chest, until her sharp teeth took a quick bite at his shoulder.

Matt pulled his hands back from behind Sara and ran them

down her thighs and over her knees. Her mouth found his, and their bodies were pressed together from hip to mouth.

Sara pulled away, sitting up on her knees again. With nimble fingers, she pulled his briefs down, releasing his hard shaft. She leaned back over him, trapping his throbbing penis between them. She rubbed her body against his, sending waves of excitement through him.

Matt wrapped his arms around Sara, holding her tight. Sara was ready, he knew it, could feel it in the heat of her body. He drew in a deep breath, sharp with her musk. The ache in his groin told him he was ready, too. But Sara had taken charge.

Sara rocked her hips against Matt. Her fingers dug into his shoulders, then trailed up to hold his head, and she covered his mouth with hers.

She held his bottom lip in her teeth, sucking and licking. She pulled his tongue deep in her mouth. His hands gripped her hips, and she rocked against him once again.

Matt could feel himself swelling, stretching, until he thought he would burst. Sara was driving him wild. He pressed himself against her.

"Not yet." Sara chuckled deep in her throat. "Not yet."

"Why not?" Matt's voice cracked. He wanted her so badly he could hardly speak.

"Because I said so." Sitting back up, she took his shaft in her hand. Matt groaned and pushed himself hard into her hand. She ran her other hand over his body, tickling his navel, running her fingertips across the sensitive skin under his arms. He bucked and moaned, unable to control his reactions. She was in control, teasing him and torturing him, driving him crazy with desire. He could hear her deep chuckle, the warm sound that told him she knew exactly what she was doing.

Two could play that game. His hands roamed over her, pinching her nipples, squeezing her breasts, stroking the sensitive skin under her arm. He ran a finger along the underside of her breast, and felt her shudder in response. She was breathing in short gasps, as though she could not get enough air.

His hand skimmed lower, and he could feel the soft down of her belly tickling his palm. Lower still, and springy curls rubbed his palm. Sara arched her hips, shoving herself against his hand.

With a swift movement, Matt reached out one finger and ran it along her cleft, plunging it deep inside her, then retreating just as fast. He could feel her muscles tighten around him as he withdrew, feel her need.

Her hands continued to stroke him, but now there was an increased urgency in her touch. She squeezed and stroked, gripping him tightly. Matt gritted his teeth, forcing himself to wait a little longer.

He continued stroking her, teasing her, then plunging deep inside her. Sara bucked, her back arching, her hips rising to meet his touch. He could feel the hard nub of her clitoris hidden deep in her folds, and he grasped it gently between his fingertips. He rubbed slightly, and Sara began to quiver. He knew she was near the peak, and he stilled his hands, holding her at the top, feeling her vibrate with need. She began to relax slightly, the tension receding.

She was stroking him hard and fast, as though he was inside her. He rubbed again, and she was instantly shaking. The nub in his fingertips pulsed and throbbed, moving against his fingers even though Sara was still. Her fingers clutched his shaft, and her body would not wait any longer.

Matt drew his hand away. Sara released him, raising herself on her knees.

Pausing every few seconds, she lowered herself over him. He slid between her swollen lips, then quivered there as she stopped. She groaned with pleasure. Her hands were clenched around his, holding them, and he could feel the throbbing of her lips around him. She lowered herself a little further, and groaned again. He slid through a ring of muscle that instantly tightened around him. At last, with one sharp movement, she lowered herself to meet him.

A sigh escaped his lips, relief at the pleasure so long denied. He lay still for a moment, staring into Sara's eyes, seeing in them a hunger that matched his own. He rocked his hips, and Sara responded, her walls tightening around him, holding him deep inside her.

She raised and lowered her body, her muscles tightening around him. She was moaning now, begging without words for release.

She lowered herself and ground against his crotch, whimpering with need. Matt pushed up into her, felt one last spasm, and then he heard her deep, open-throated cry of completion. She rocked against him, her breath harsh and ragged. Her hips relaxed, and her muscles were no longer rigid around him.

Her eyes were wide in the dark, and Matt could see little else. He rocked again, and he could feel himself growing, swelling. He tried to retreat, to draw out the moment, but it was no use. Sara was tight around him, holding him, and he could feel the slow pulsing of her diminishing climax squeezing him.

The pressure was more than he could take. She pulsed again, and Matt was lost. He heard himself cry out, and then he was swept away on a wave of pleasure, and he lost himself in the sensation.

The boat rocked, and Matt felt Sara move over him with the roll of the deck. She sighed, lowered herself next to him and settled into his arms, their bodies cooling in the night air.

Matt knew that soon they would have to find clothes, to cover themselves for protection from the chill, but he wanted to delay as long as possible. Sara was content, relaxed in his arms, and he savored the feel of her skin on his.

In the darkness around them he could hear the sound of small nocturnal animals. The surf pounded at the entrance to the river, and gentle waves slapped at the sides of the boat. For a little while, he was able to forget his problems.

Until he heard the unmistakable sound of a diesel engine, echoing between the rocky cliffs.

Chapter 27

Matt groaned. It wasn't over. There could be thousands of boats on the ocean, but somehow he knew that this was the one boat he didn't want to see.

He hated to disturb Sara, but he nudged her, and she jerked awake. It was dark, and he couldn't see her face, but he could feel the tension in her body. He knew the moment she heard the engine.

"We have to move," she whispered. "Now!"

Matt helped her find her discarded jeans and shirt, and let her pull him to his feet.

He could walk, though not well. He still leaned heavily on Sara as they made their way to the wheelhouse. The radio had found something, and he could hear the exchange between two voices that he recognized.

"I cannot sail through that passage. It is too shallow. Therefore, you must go. Take care of the problem." The captain's stilted English didn't hide the chilling intent of his words. They were the problem, and the captain wanted Harry to "take care" of them.

"Hey, comrade," Harry's voice was defiant. "I checked three harbors and a bunch of inlets for you. If they're in here, it's up to you to fix it. I've done my part, more than my part, and I am outta here."

The signal was weak, both boats transmitting on extremely low power, limiting the range of their broadcast. Neither one expected to be overheard.

"This is your problem also, Mr. Yost. The Coast Guard will be most interested in the activities of an American fishing boat with a large amount of cash and no fish."

"Alex, if they was gonna call the Guard, they'd have done it by now. We haven't seen anything. So either they don't know shit, or their radio's busted. Either way, you take care of the problem and I'm not even here.

"So long, comrade. Let's not do this again, okay?"

Matt stood with his arm around Sara. He could feel her trembling as she listened to the exchange between Harry and the man he called Alex. Harry would run, and hope for the best. Alex, whoever he was, wasn't going to give up.

They were in deep shit, and they had to get themselves out.

"First thing," Matt said. "Get me some pants. Please. I'm freezing my ass off."

He felt Sara's spine stiffen under his arm. Without question or hesitation, she dropped down the ladder, returning in seconds with sweats and heavy socks.

They were safe for the moment. *Ludmilla* couldn't get up the river, Alex had said so. But it was only a matter of time before something had to give. They couldn't stay hidden forever, and the smugglers weren't good at waiting.

Sara pulled the sweat pants on him while he balanced against the chart table, then covered his feet with the socks. Just putting a sock on his injured ankle ignited hot coals of pain under the surface. Matt bit the inside of his cheek, digging his teeth into the soft surface to keep from crying out.

She adjusted the stool, and he rested his leg on it. He was stable, if not comfortable. He could pilot, but he wouldn't be much good if they were boarded.

"Sara." He pulled her to him, and held her close. Her hair still smelled of sea and sun, and she was warm in his arms. He had a sense of a faint memory, and realized he was storing pieces of Sara, just like he did when he left on a trip.

He held her for a minute longer, then released her. "They don't know we heard them. Harry thinks the radio's out. He's half-right. And Alex, whoever he is, can't get the trawler up the river. But I don't think he's a very patient man."

Sara nodded, her head rubbing against his chest. He squeezed her tight, then released her. "We can't do this alone. We have to activate the emergency beacon."

Chapter 28

Sara nodded in agreement. This was an undeniable emergency, and they had to call for help. "Okay," she said. "What do I do?"

Matt pointed to the small radio transmitter, mounted out of the way on the far corner on the helm. "Just switch it on. The satellite will pick up the signal and do the rest."

She wanted to believe it was that easy. She flipped the switch, and a small red light began to blink. The pulsing light filled the wheelhouse with an eerie stop-and-go red glow. With each pulse she could almost see Matt's face, but it was like being in a bad disco. The light was too dim to really see, and then just as her eyes adjusted to it, it flickered off again. The overall effect left her stomach rolling unpleasantly.

She pulled a sweatshirt over her T-shirt and tied her hair back. She was ready for whatever came.

The blinking continued, and Sara couldn't stand it any longer. She grabbed a rag and covered the light. It didn't eliminate the pulsing in the wheelhouse, but it settled her stomach.

"How long will it take them?" she asked.

"Don't know for sure." Matt put an arm around her shoulders, and held her. "Twenty or thirty minutes, maybe. Whatever the chopper flying time is from *Astoria*. The beacon's registered, they know who we are, and," he chuckled a little at the thought, "they already know our radio doesn't work, even if they don't know when it broke."

She sighed and hugged herself to Matt. She wondered if that would be too long. She knew too long would be however long it took Alex and his crew to devise a way to come after them.

The radio had fallen silent, and the cove held an eerie quiet. Even the nocturnal animals seemed to have disappeared. Sara felt brittle with tension, as though she could shatter into a million pieces. The waiting was impossible. She wanted something to happen. Now.

Her wish was answered, to her horror, by the whine of an outboard motor at the mouth of the river. Her heart leaped into her throat, and ice water flooded her veins.

It was far too soon for the Coast Guard.

Sara remembered seeing a dinghy suspended on *Ludmilla*'s fore deck. They must have launched it when Harry turned tail.

"They launched the dinghy," Matt said, echoing her thoughts. His hand tightened on her shoulder. "Do you know how many of them there were?"

Sara squeezed her eyes shut and concentrated on recalling the images of last night. It seemed a lifetime ago, but it was only a matter of hours.

"Four. At least, that's all I ever saw. The young guy and the one with the knife who were fighting, the guy with the bottle, and the captain." She didn't add that the captain had the gun. She didn't need to.

"One of them would have to stay with the boat, but there might be all three of the others in the dinghy. I think it was big enough."

Sara swallowed hard, and nodded.

"Can you cast off that line?" Matt asked.

"I don't know. I snagged the tree and pulled it tight."

"Cut it if you have to. If there's three of 'em in the dinghy, there's only one on the trawler. If that's the case, I can get us out of here."

Matt's hands were on the controls, checking the settings and the instruments. He turned on a tiny light over the table, and peered closely at the charts. "We're close enough to make port before they can get back on board and follow us."

● ● ●

Sara thought she heard "I hope" in Matt's tone, but he didn't say it. She had to believe they could reach safety, and act accordingly. If she didn't believe him, they were already lost.

She swallowed the lump in her throat. "When?"

Matt took a last look at the instruments and turned to her. He kissed her hard on the mouth, and squeezed her bottom. "Now," he said quietly.

Sara grabbed the knife she had used earlier, and went aft. She tied off to the jack line, knowing the boat could move erratically when she cut the line.

The diesels roared to life, and she swung the knife high over her head. In one swift stroke she severed the line that held them. *Excelsior* surged forward as the current caught her, and Sara could feel the battle for control between Matt and the river.

Sara sheathed the knife, and stuck the sheath through her belt. It was awkward, but it was a weapon, and she felt better knowing she had it.

By the time she reached the wheelhouse, Matt was switching on the two halogen searchlights on top of the wheelhouse. He played them across the river, their beams cutting a narrow path of brilliance through the black night.

The light caught the dinghy in its glowing eye. Sara tried to make out the men in the tiny craft. The man with the knife was there, and his younger look-alike.

There was a sharp noise, and one of the two lights exploded, raining broken glass onto the deck. The smugglers were shooting at them!

Matt doused the other light, removing the smugglers' target. In the dim glow from the chart light, Sara saw him reach below the wheel and pull out the flare gun.

They were pulling into the channel from the relative calm of the tiny cove. Sara remembered the difficulty she had, and she knew it would take all Matt's skill and attention to get them out.

She grabbed the flare gun from his hand, and dropped spare cartridges in her pocket.

"Not in the air," Matt said through gritted teeth. "Shoot at the sons-of-bitches."

Sara didn't stop to answer. She stepped cautiously out of the wheelhouse, the flare gun clenched in both hands. *Excelsior* was rocking in the current, and she stumbled.

She reached out a hand to steady herself. She grabbed the safety line. Though she didn't trust her entire weight to the thin line, it gave her time to recover her balance. She drew a deep breath, and braced her legs on the rolling deck. She had gained her sea legs over the past couple days, and now was the time to prove it.

She could hear the whine of the outboard, but it echoed off the water and was swallowed in the dense trees that stood on either side of the river. She wasn't sure where they were.

"Sara!" Matt's voice hissed out of the darkness behind her. "Get ready."

"Now!"

The remaining searchlight sent a beacon across the river, and caught the dinghy in its beam. The younger man was crouched in the bow, the gun in his hand resting on the gunwale. Behind him, the older man held the tiller on the outboard.

The light went out again before he could get off a shot. But Sara's target was larger, and Matt's warning had allowed her to aim in the instant the light was on.

She pulled the trigger.

The unexpected shock of the recoil knocked her off balance. She staggered back and sat down on the deck. She missed the hatch cover, but banged her elbow against a latch. Numbing bolts of electricity shot up and down from the elbow, and her arm would not bend.

The flare streaked across the river, trailing orange colored smoke behind it. It hit the side of the dinghy with a thud, and fell into the water. She could see the faint glow as it sank below the surface, and the bubbles of smoke that rose to the top and burst around the dinghy.

Sara tucked the flare gun under her arm, and reached for another round, as Matt once more shot the searchlight beam at the dinghy. It was surrounded by a cloud of orange smoke, and the men on board were choking on the fumes.

Somehow, the longhaired man managed to raise his gun, firing directly at the wheelhouse. At Matt. Sara froze in terror and her heart raced.

She heard the bullet tear into the wooden side of the wheelhouse. He had missed Matt, but she couldn't let him have another shot.

"No more light," she called to Matt.

The sparks in her elbow had subsided, and she raised the flare gun. She aimed where she thought the dinghy was, and fired a second flare.

The trail of smoke burrowed into the orange cloud. Sara heard a scream of pain from inside the cloud, but she couldn't tell which man it was, or what had happened. She hoped it was the young man and his damned gun.

An orange glow appeared in the middle of the smoke cloud, and the screaming grew louder. The glow grew brighter, and appeared to move in a dozen directions at once. Suddenly it moved in a straight line and disappeared, accompanied by a loud splash.

The screaming stopped.

Sara struggled with the images that her imagination created. The flare had landed in the dinghy. It had hurt someone. Something had fallen in the water.

No, someone had fallen in the water. A guilty rush of joy flooded through her. She had evened up the odds a little.

The cloud of smoke swirled. She couldn't really see the dinghy, but she could see where its passage disturbed the smoke cloud. They were still coming, headed for *Excelsior*.

Sara had one flare left in her pocket, but they might need it to signal the Coast Guard. She held her breath for a moment, straining to hear the hoped-for sound of a helicopter.

All she heard was the whine of the approaching outboard.

Matt had cleared the cove and they were in the main channel of the river now. Ahead of them in the dark was the dinghy. Somewhere in the river was the man who had gone overboard. Beyond that the trawler waited for them, in the dark.

The dinghy drew closer. Another shot slammed into the wheelhouse.

Dammit! She hadn't hit him. Or maybe they both had guns. It didn't matter. Someone was shooting.

The dinghy sounded like it was nearly on top of them. She could hear the shouted curses of the man over the sounds of the motor.

The dinghy slid past them in the dark. The voice receded. The outboard motor raced, and she sensed that he were turning back, trying to come alongside.

Matt threw the engines in reverse, jerking her hard against the jack line. She hung on, cursing.

Excelsior strained at the sudden change, then slowed. She hung motionless for long seconds. Her diesels throbbed, vibrating the deck under Sara's feet.

Matt was chasing the dinghy up the river, in reverse!
Sara clung to the jack line as *Excelsior* churned backward. She could hear excited shouts coming from up the river, and the whine of the outboard motor.

The dinghy shot past her in the dark. She heard the two hulls scrape against each other, then the dinghy raced back toward the mouth of the river.

A bullet shattered one of the wheelhouse windows. Sara's heart stopped, and she held her breath.

Seconds later, *Excelsior* reversed direction again. Matt was in control. Her heart started beating again, and she drew a deep breath.

They would pay. For the night of terror, and the day of running. For the gut-wrenching fear. But most of all for trying to hurt Matt.

They raced toward the dinghy. *Excelsior* gained speed, and Matt seemed intent on reaching the mouth of the river, no matter what the obstacles.

The dinghy cut in front of them, a shadow in the pale light of the rising moon. Matt yelled, and increased the throttle.

With a sickening crunch, *Excelsior* plowed into the tiny craft. The screams of the man in the boat mixed with the splintering of wood and the crunch of metal. The outboard's whine climbed as it was freed from the drag of the water, then died as it plunged below the surface.

Splintered boards flew over *Excelsior*'s bow. Sara heard a window shatter. Matt threw the diesels into reverse, and slowed the boat to a crawl.

The searchlight cut across the water. Wreckage littered the river from one bank to the other, and debris rode the current toward the ocean.

Sara couldn't see any of the crew. Then she spotted a body floating near the shore. As the searchlight passed over it, she caught a glimpse of dark hair. Her stomach turned over as she realized it wasn't the man's hair she was looking at — it was his narrow face, burned and blackened. The searchlight swung on around, leaving the image of the charred face stamped into her brain.

Excelsior was moving toward the mouth of the river, plowing her way through the rubble. The stern of the dinghy slid past, now little more than a transom board floating in the dark water. Pale moonlight caught a piece of metal, and it glistened for a moment before sliding beneath the water.

After the noise of the past few minutes, the quiet drew Sara's nerves even tighter. No more shots whizzed past her to bury themselves in the walls of the wheelhouse. No windows shattered. The outboard motor was silenced, and *Excelsior*'s diesels were running slow as she made for the mouth of the river.

Sara looked toward the mouth of the river. The lighted bulk of the trawler slid into view in the narrow gap. They were trying to block the river. A shadow passed across the lighted silhouette, and in the momentary silence Sara heard Harry Yost's shout from the radio.

"... I can't let you ..."

There was a sickening crunch. The lights of the trawler wavered, and she heeled over. As Sara watched, a wave caught her and swept her away from the narrow opening.

Harry's voice crackled from the radio again. "Matt, if you can hear me, I was never here. I couldn't let him do it, but you didn't see me, Matt. That trawler ran onto the rocks by herself." His voice cracked with desperation. He was begging. "For God's sake, Matt. Please! I'll explain when we get home."

Sara saw a shadow pass across the mouth of the river again, and she imagined Harry and the rest of the crew, desperate and frightened. She hoped they would be clear before the Coast Guard arrived.

Chapter 29

Sara felt, more than heard, the scraping against the hull. She thought another piece of debris had come alongside, and she bent over the gunwale to fend it off.

The man's knife was gripped in his teeth. He clung to the severed end of the anchor line with one hand, and grabbed for Sara with the other.

His wet, gray hair was plastered against his head, and his eyes were unfocused. His long fingers closed around Sara's wrist, pulling her close to his face.

He was growling. A harsh, angry sound deep in his throat. He stared at Sara, through her, as though he was looking at someone else far behind her.

There were no words, just guttural noises through clenched teeth. He reached for the knife with the hand that held the rope. He kept the other clamped around Sara's wrist.

She was being pulled over the transom. Her feet touched the deck, but she could feel herself inching overboard. She tried to find a purchase with her toes, some way to brace herself against the steady pull of the man in the water.

He fumbled with the knife, trying to get a grip on it without letting go of Sara or the rope. The blade seemed impossibly huge as it wavered in front of her face, occasional beams of moonlight glinting off its dull surface.

She wanted to scream for help, but her throat refused to open. All that came out were breathy noises, lost in the quiet throbbing of the diesels.

The old man's growling and gibberish came into sharp focus for an instant. His eyes locked on hers, filled with hatred. He spoke a single English word. "Brother." Then he resumed his growling.

In the distance, a new noise beat its way into Sara's brain. A steady thumping came washing over the cliffs. Her heart leaped with joy. A helicopter. Rescue. Safety.

The old man tugged on her wrist, and she slipped a little farther. She caught her knee under the gunwale, and dug in. She had to hold on.

He held the knife in his hand, and shifted his grip. Brought it up to strike at her.

The searchlight of the helicopter washed over them. For the first time, he noticed the noise. Looked in the direction of the light.

Sara didn't think. She acted. The distraction was enough. She yanked her wrist from his grip, and lunged back into the boat, landing hard on her hip.

As she scrambled to her feet, the arm with the knife snaked over the transom. He was pulling himself up the stub of rope that trailed behind them.

The rope lay taut on the transom, the man's hands reaching up to gain another few inches. She pulled her knife from its sheath and raised it over her head.

She screamed with all the anger and frustration, all the pent-up emotions of the last twenty-four hours, and brought the knife down across the transom.

Her scream was answered by another from the water. The old man tumbled away from the boat, cut free of *Excelsior* by her blow.

Shaking, Sara collapsed to the deck. Tears ran from her eyes, and her breath came in great convulsive sobs. The light of the helicopter shone on her, and a deep voice boomed down.

"Vessel *Excelsior*, this is the Coast Guard. Just stay where you are. We're coming for you."

Chapter 30

The captain of the Coast Guard ship stood in the wheelhouse with Matt and Sara. There wasn't enough room for all three of them, but Matt hadn't let Sara leave his side since he found her curled against the transom, crying hysterically.

"We saw them last night," he glanced at the cold dawn outside the broken windows, "night before last, in Pelican Bay," Matt said.

The captain nodded at him. "Go on."

"We thought they were just lost." Sara nodded, and he hugged her close. He wanted her where he could touch her, assure himself she was really okay.

"They had a big fight," she said. "That's when we decided to leave."

"They had guns." Matt waved a hand toward the shattered glass of the wheelhouse. "Obviously."

The captain turned to Matt and fixed him with a cold stare. Matt could feel the steel in that look, and he winced inwardly.

"Mr. Carpenter, there is still the issue of filing a false report. If you had given us your true location, we might have been able to save you and your wife a lot of grief."

It was Matt's turn to shrug. "Maybe so. But I did what I thought was best. I was out here, I saw what was happening, and I tried to protect both of us."

He squeezed Sara's shoulder, and she lay her hand on his. Her fingers closed over his, a warm, reassuring touch. "We both decided, captain. We did what we thought was best," she lied in her sweetest, most innocent voice. "I was terrified."

"You seem to have recovered," the captain said dryly.

Sara's fingers squeezed Matt's hand, but her face remained clear and open. "I did what I had to do. He was trying to kill me." She shivered, and frowned for a minute, looking up at the captain. "Do you know who they were? The crewmen, I mean?"

Matt admired the skill with which she had changed the subject. This Sara was full of surprises, and he looked forward to finding them all.

"Yeah, we know them. Like I said, we've been trying to catch them. The captain is Aleksandr Rezhnenko, and the other one who stayed behind is Krushkin. The two in the dinghy were the Petrov brothers, Ivan and Pytor."

"That explains it," Sara said quietly.

"Explains what?" the captain asked.

"He said one word that I understood. 'Brother.' Now I know why." She shuddered.

The captain stuck his hand out to Matt. The two men shook hands in the shattered wreckage of the wheelhouse. Then the captain extended his hand to Sara.

"Thank you both for your help." He looked around once more, his glance covering the broken glass, shattered doorways, and splintered wood surrounding the bullet holes. "There is a reward. It's not a lot, but it should more than cover the repairs."

The captain turned and left the wheelhouse. He paused just before he stepped off onto the dock and looked back over his shoulder. "If you ever get tired of chasing fish," he said, "come and see me. We can always use people like you." He stopped and looked straight at Sara. "Both of you."

He stepped onto the dock and walked away.

Matt looked down at his wife. There were dark circles under her eyes, fatigue pulled at the corners of her mouth, and her hands were red and rough. She looked good enough to eat.
"Well, what do you think of that offer?" he asked.

"Flattering." She turned to look deep in Matt's eyes. "But I think I have a job, don't I?"

"Sure," Matt said, and kissed her. "Now let's go home." He patted his shirt pocket to make sure the processor's check for their catch was still there, and pressed the starter.

Sara cast off the lines and came back to the wheelhouse. She stood close to him, her soft breast pressing against his arm. "Let's go," she said. "You know, I think I learned a few things this trip."

Matt nodded, concentrating on pulling away from the dock. They both had.

Sara chuckled. In a husky voice that brought all his attention back to her, she added, "If you're lucky, I just might show you some of them."